It was a harmless fantasy

Charity imagined herself on Venice Beach, lying on the sun-warmed sand.

Instead of her winter-weight wool police uniform, she was clad in a yellow bikini—skimpier than any she'd ever dared wear—soaking up the golden rays of the sun while a handsome man, wearing tight white tennis shorts and no shirt, rubbed sunblock all over her body.

She sighed as his wide, clever hands stroked their way across her shoulders, down her back, along the soft skin at the inside of her thighs, spreading oil and sensual warmth at the same time. She heard the ebb and flow of the tide, the soft sigh of the summer breeze, the ringing of bells.

Bells?

Jerked back to reality, back to the Maine blizzard raging outside, Charity grabbed the telephone receiver muttering, ''I hope it's not another crackpot complaint about UFO sightings.''

Dear Reader,

"Second to the right, and then straight on till morning." Peter Pan's words capture the human spirit at its most adventurous—the desire to find out what's around the next corner. JoAnn Ross has taken this same determination and crafted two wonderful love stories that we just had to make Editor's Choice books. *Star-Crossed Lovers* has the magic of two *very* different people falling in love, while #436 *Moonstruck Lovers,* available next month, takes us on a rollicking space adventure.

This is what Temptation does best—break a few barriers to give you the most contemporary, sensual romances possible. Nineteen-ninety-three continues to be an exciting year with our Lovers & Legends miniseries, and more Editor's Choice novels including a sizzling hot story by Mallory Rush in June called *Love Slave* (need we say more?). Glenda Sanders's ghost trilogy concludes with *Lovers Secrets,* available this summer.

And yes, "Second to the right, and then straight on till morning," were also Captain Kirk's last words in *Star Trek VI.*

Enjoy!

Birgit Davis-Todd
Senior Editor

P.S. JoAnn would love to hear from her readers. Write to her:

JoAnn Ross
c/o Harlequin Temptation
225 Duncan Mill Road
Don Mills, Ontario
M3B 3K9

STAR-CROSSED LOVERS

JoAnn Ross

Harlequin Books

TORONTO • NEW YORK • LONDON
AMSTERDAM • PARIS • SYDNEY • HAMBURG
STOCKHOLM • ATHENS • TOKYO • MILAN
MADRID • WARSAW • BUDAPEST • AUCKLAND

Published February 1993

ISBN 0-373-25532-2

STAR-CROSSED LOVERS

1

The planet Sarnia
Moon date: Gamma 17.3

THERE WAS NO TURNING BACK.

After studying the holotapes in the secret government archives, after charting and recharting his destination, after spending five long solar revolutions designing and constructing his transporter, Sarnian astrophysicist and hopeful intergalactic explorer Bram Starbuck was on his way.

Lights—red, green, yellow and blue flashed behind his closed lids. The light was a medley of wavelengths, surrounding him, radiating in all directions. His body felt as if it were being stung by a hundred, a thousand, angry nitrowasps.

Employing the centuries-old meditation techniques the Ancient Ones had brought with them from the planet Janos on Stratum Eleven, Starbuck focused his thoughts, directing his mind to his destination: the planet Earth in the Milky Way galaxy.

Starbuck had chosen Earth because its atmosphere and gravitational pull were remarkably similar to that of Sarnia. Also, although he'd been a child at the time, he could remember in vivid detail the excursion he'd taken with his parents and sister in the family spacecraft.

The occasion had been the quatercentenary of his mother's homeland and although four hundred years of a nation's existence was a mere blink of an eyelash to a Sarnian, the Americans, his mother included, had considered it quite an accomplishment.

Starbuck had chosen California for his destination because he remembered the southern state in North America to be a harmonious and eclectic location. Venice, specifically, he recalled, was a place where a stranger's sudden appearance amidst the amazingly diverse mix of natives would not cause alarm.

There was another reason he'd chosen Earth as his destination. A highly inappropriate, vastly un-Sarnian, particularly human, emotional reason.

This trip was a personal pilgrimage to the planet of his mother's birth. And although hope was heretically antireason and entirely irrational—therefore diametrically opposed to every aspect of Sarnian philosophy—in some dark secret place inside his heart, Starbuck hoped that somehow, by understanding the planet his mother had willingly left behind but had never forgotten, he might come to understand himself.

In preparation for his journey, his mother had told him everything about her planet that she could remember. Unfortunately, with the exception of that one visit, Rachel Valderian had been away from her home for more than forty years. Starbuck needed more detailed, up-to-date information than she could provide.

Although it was technically against confederation regulations, Sarnian government officials had found an arcane loophole in the intergalaxy treaty and placed, out of sensor range, intelligence satellites whose cloaking devices had allowed them to go unnoticed around earth.

For more than one hundred solar revolutions, the satellites had been beaming back pictures and audio tapes of the planet Earth.

Scores of clerks—females, whose duty it was to handle the mundane, mindless tasks that were the hallmark of government bureaucracies throughout the universe—transferred the electronic data onto holotapes, which were filed away in the government archives.

Starbuck's sister Julianna, a highly placed government xenoanthropologist and the sole female professor at the Sarnian Science Institute, had originally professed grave doubts about both Starbuck's theory and his motive.

When she couldn't convince him to give up his dangerous plan, Julianna relented and, risking her own career, provided him with classified government datachips far more detailed than the holofiles he'd been permitted to check out from the Sarnian National Library.

This wealth of information enabled Starbuck to learn the language and customs of the place called California.

And now, utilizing his unproven theory of molecular astro-projection, Starbuck intended to be the first intergalactic traveler without the protection—and encumbrance—of a space vehicle.

Julianna was seated at the computer, her expression grave as her fingers tapped over the touch-plate, turning complex mathematical algorithms into scientific visualization.

Her pale-blond hair was arranged atop her head in its usual tidy braided coronet and she was wearing a softly clinging silvery blue gown, the patch that revealed her to be a fifth-level Academician on her breast.

Although everything about his sister—her hair, her classically styled gown, her studious demeanor—was carefully calculated to portray formal restraint, an aura of un-Sarnian excitement surrounded her like a shimmering alpha field.

Outside the clear quartzalite windows, moonlight cast a rosy glow over Sarnia. Inside, Starbuck and Julianna watched the amber monitor as the computer scanned its way through billions of miles and thousands of light-years.

Four-dimensional visuals of the universe burst forth in a dazzling display of furious fireworks: stars flaring, dying in cold black voids while worlds were being reborn from exploded remnants, whirling galaxies hurling heated gases in all directions, glittering stardust, blinding fireballs and speeding, spinning, flaming quasars.

Planets were scattered about like comet-tail dust over thousands of light-years; matter and light disappeared, sucked up by devouring black holes, disappearing from the screen, never to be seen again.

"We're coming up on the Milky Way," Julianna announced unnecessarily as the glowing, spiraling band of starlight appeared on the screen.

That shared feeling of expectation was practically making the air crackle around them. It crossed Starbuck's mind that he could use a Valdox.

Not that he would have resorted to taking one of the popular tranquilizer tabs. Because if there was ever a time when he needed to keep all his wits about him, this was definitely it.

Spiral arms extended outward from the mass of light, like an Earth child's pinwheel.

A pleasant, long-ago memory flashed through his mind. Starbuck's lips curved into a faint smile as he recalled his mother purchasing the whimsical red-and-white toy for him at some fantastical kingdom terrans had inexplicably named Disneyland.

His memory of that halcyon afternoon was as clear as if it had been yesterday. He could feel the warmth of his mother's gaze, smell the evocative scent she always wore, the perfumed oil created from the moonflowers she cultivated in her greenhouse garden. That same scent was repeated in the potpourri Rachel Valderian had insisted on keeping in every room of their home.

And although none of his friends' mothers would have ever done anything so frivolous as growing flowers, Starbuck had secretly thought them wonderful. Indeed, he could never think of his mother without seeing those bright red blooms.

His smile turned to a frown as he also remembered returning to Sarnia and having Hotek Venturian, a mean-spirited green-blooded Sarnian boy take the pinwheel away and crush it beneath the heel of his crokogator-skin boot.

Nothing was free, Starbuck had learned. Eidetic memory, as useful as it was, did not come without its own high cost. All experiences—good and bad—were automatically, indelibly stored in his memory banks, waiting only to be recalled.

Starbuck sighed and returned his attention to Julianna's screen, studying the glowing orb inside one of the galaxy's spiral arms.

He and his sister exchanged a meaningful look. The glorious flaring body was Earth's sun.

"It won't be long now," he said.

Julianna's lovely face, schooled since infancy to appear serene, was anything but. Her normally smooth pale brow was furrowed, her clear amber eyes—a legacy from their mother—revealed inappropriate concern, and worry lines bracketed her lips.

"There's still time to change your mind," she advised him.

Starbuck didn't answer. There was no need. Although Julianna was mindblind, lacking Sarnian telepathy, he knew that it was not necessary for her to read his mind to know what he was thinking. Because she also possessed the terran blood of their mother, his sister could appreciate the driving need that had gnawed at Starbuck for as long as he could remember.

From this vantage point, Starbuck was able to see all the planets: Pluto, a brief speck, seen, then dismissed. Icy Neptune, with its eight moons and clouds of methane ice; blue shrouded Uranus with its twin moons, Oberon and Titania; enormous, stormy Jupiter; beringed Saturn and Mars, its dark red landscape appearing, from this distance, so like his own planet.

Then there she was. Earth.

Starbuck's studies allowed him to recognize the land masses floating in the blue seas, the glittering white of the polar ice caps, the jagged snow-topped ridges of the Himalayas, the Alps, the Andes, the Cascades, the Rockies.

He drew in a breath and leaned forward, taking in a thin gray ribbon that curled across the Asian landscape, and realized that he was looking at the Great Wall of China. He remembered his mother telling him the enormous man-made barricade had been erected to repel intruders, but at the time, he'd been too young to fully comprehend the concept of armed, deadly enemies.

Sarnia had been peaceful for generations. Indeed, it had been more than six hundred solar revolutions since his planet had experienced war.

Starbuck's heart picked up its beat as he stepped into the imaging circle. He tightened his fingers around the compact quantum accelerator. It had taken years of fine-tuning, but he'd finally succeeded in shrinking the molecular accelerator down to a size small enough to be held in a man's palm. It was also small enough to include a miniature ecumenical translator. The voice module for the translator was implanted in his middle ear. No properly prepared space traveler would think of leaving Sarnia without his ecumenical translator or his hologram credit disk.

Starbuck concentrated all his energies on his extrasensory perception, one of the few genetic traits he shared with other Sarnians. In order to fully understand the people who populated his mother's planet, he must appear to be one of them. If he were to walk among the inhabitants of Earth without drawing undue attention to himself, he must make certain that his features blended harmoniously with the natives.

And since his own clothing was created from fabrics not available on Earth and fashioned in current Sarnian style, he needed to ensure that he was properly attired. For that, he required a model drawn from the mind of a terran.

Utilizing the mental imaging that was as natural to every Sarnian as breathing, Starbuck imagined he could feel the warmth of the sun on his body, he could hear the ebb and flow of the Pacific Ocean tide along the Venice, California, shoreline. He could smell the salt on the warm summer breeze.

Sounds rose up from the spinning blue-green orb that was Earth, reverberating inharmoniously in his ear like voices from the ancient Tower of Bukh.

Images flashed before his eyes like a laserfilm, glowing in the shimmering, ghostly beam of white light.

He had just managed to separate one feminine Earthling's thoughts from the others when Julianna's startled voice interrupted his concentration.

"What do you mean we miscalculated?" he shouted as he was pulled faster and faster toward the light.

Starbuck felt a pulsing deep inside his body, the increasingly strong beats synchronizing with the flashing lights that were now the entire spectrum of the rainbow.

He was breaking apart. Disintegrating. Dissolving in the sparkling golden light.

"And where the sweet nirvana is Castle Mountain, Maine?"

It was the last thing Starbuck would say before vanishing from his laboratory.

And his planet.

*Castle Mountain Island,
Maine January 17*

IT HAD BEEN SNOWING for five days.

More than twenty inches of the wet white stuff had been dumped on Castle Mountain and if the weather forecast was even close to the mark, another ten inches would pile up before the series of storms, dubbed the Canadian Express, had passed.

Although she'd grown up on the remote island off the rocky Maine coast, six years spent in Southern California had made Charity forget how cold her home state could get.

She poured a cup of coffee into a chipped mug, sank down into the leather chair, put her booted feet up on the scarred old desk that, like the chair, had belonged to her father, blew on the coffee to cool it and watched the white flakes of snow being blown against the window.

Even as she reminded herself that she'd grown bored with California's unrelenting sunshine and that her nostalgic desire for seasonal changes had been one of her reasons for deciding to leave the Venice, California, police force to pin on her father's badge here in Castle Mountain, Charity hoped the snow would let up long enough for her to drive home.

Leaning her head against the back of the chair, she closed her eyes and allowed her mind to drift. She imagined herself back on Venice Beach, lying on the sun-warmed sand in front of her rented bungalow.

Instead of the unappealing, dark blue winter-weight wool uniform she was currently wearing, in her fantasy she was clad in a yellow bikini—skimpier than she'd ever actually dared wear—soaking up the golden rays of the sun while a movie-star-handsome man, wearing tight white tennis shorts and no shirt, rubbed sun block all over her body.

She sighed as she imagined his wide, clever hands stroking their way across her shoulders, down her back, along the soft skin at the inside of her thighs, spreading oil and sensual warmth at the same time.

When he turned her in his arms, a lock of sun-bleached blond hair fell over his mahogany forehead and Charity pictured herself reaching up to brush it away.

No. Not blond, she corrected. Steve had blond hair, and if there was one person she definitely didn't want to invite into her daydreams, it was her former husband.

He'd be dark, she decided. The man of her dreams would have hair as black as midnight. And his eyes would be dark, as well, the color of obsidian, only softer. His nose wouldn't be pug, like Steve's, but strong and straight as an arrow.

His lips would be full but firmly cut, not the least bit feminine, and always tinged with a private smile just for her. Focusing on those enticing lips before moving down to take in his bold jaw, Charity drifted back into her fantasy.

She drank in the tropical scent of the coconut oil his dark hands were rubbing on her body. She heard the ebb and flow of the tide, the soft sigh of the salt-tinged summer breeze, the ringing of bells.

Bells?

Jerked back to reality again, Charity dropped her feet to the floor and grabbed up the receiver.

"Police department. Oh, hi, Dylan." There was a smile in her voice as she greeted her brother. "Don't you dare tell me you're not coming to dinner. Not when I've gone to all the trouble to fix your favorite. That's right, Grandmother Prescott's pot roast."

She laughed off her twin brother's professed alarm. "I'll have you know I got the recipe from Faith."

Of the three Prescott daughters, Charity's eldest sister Faith had always been the domestic one. Charity was not.

"She promises that it's foolproof, so you don't have to worry about ending up in the emergency room."

Charity lifted her feet to the desktop again, leaned back in the chair and twirled the plastic cord around her fingers.

"So, if you haven't called to back out on my pot roast, what's up? Another explosion in the brain factory?"

Dylan Prescott spent most of his waking and sleeping hours ensconced in a laboratory out in a remote site in the Maine island's woods. After meeting a few of her brilliant brother's equally brilliant but frighteningly loopy co-workers, Charity had stopped asking what they were doing.

As Dylan went on to explain the reason for his call, Charity's smile faded.

"No, I haven't heard a thing. You're the first person to call since Mr. McCarthy wanted to file a complaint against John Day's snowplow blocking his driveway. What kind of lights?"

She switched the phone to the other ear and, reaching over, switched on the police scanner. Set to the state police frequency, over the buzzing static, Charity could hear numerous voices, all claiming to have seen something strange in the sky over Castle Mountain Island.

"If one of you eggheads set off another experimental rocket without notifying me ahead of time, so help me, Dylan—"

A rapid-fire spat of denial came over the wire.

"All right. I believe you, you don't have to bite my head off. It's probably just the aurora borealis," she suggested. "I know it's a little late in the year, but the weatherman on Channel 4 said that it's because of the solar flares, and, after all, you're the one who told me the flares are what are causing so much chaos with the radio and television frequencies.

"So, although I'd love to have a spaceship land in the town square, just to liven things up around here, I don't think it's going to happen."

They both laughed, but Charity couldn't help noticing that her brother's laugh was not quite as robust as hers.

"Well, whatever it is," she decided, "there's undoubtedly a reasonable explanation. There always is."

After making him promise to drive carefully on the way to the house, she hung up.

She'd no sooner replaced the receiver than the phone rang again.

And again.

An hour later, after it seemed that she'd talked to nearly all one hundred and forty of Castle Mountain's residents, Charity was left wondering what on earth had gotten into everyone.

Their stories varied, but everyone, from the mayor to Andy Kelly—whose wood carvings had made him a celebrity among summer visitors who were willing to pay big bucks for a life-size porcupine made out of toothpicks—to Agnes Adams, the town's librarian for forty-five years, all insisted that aliens had landed on Castle Mountain Island.

The descriptions of the alleged spaceship ranged from a shimmering blue light, to a white light shaped like a cigar, to a silver saucer-shaped spaceship.

Johnny Kelly, Andy's son and paperboy for the weekly *Castle Mountain Yankee Observer*, reported that he'd seen a gang of seven-foot-tall men dressed in what looked like Reynolds Wrap walking down Main Street; seventy-nine-year-old Scott MacIntyre, who'd run the Shell station on Maple Drive since long before Charity had been born, reported that three-foot-tall little green men with single flashing eyes in the middle of their foreheads had dug a hole in the football field at Evergreen High School.

And a hysterical Mildred O'Connor, owner of Mildred's Shear Pleasures Beauty Emporium, was certain she'd seen a filmy, smokelike entity going down her neighbor's chimney.

"Do you think it could possibly be smoke coming *out* of the chimney?" Charity asked mildly. She smiled as the machine-gun-quick babble on the other end of the phone quieted. "Don't worry about it," she said after the beautician apologized for calling. "That's what I'm here for."

"It must be the full moon," she decided, after the phone had been silent for twenty minutes. "That and the flares and the storm. Five straight days of staying indoors can make anyone stir-crazy."

Charity knew it was certainly getting to her.

Making a mental note to ask Dylan if he knew of any instances where solar flares had caused mass hallucinations, she pulled on her gloves, put on her sheepskin-lined coat, switched the telephone to ring at her house and strode through the drifting snow to her four-wheel-drive Jeep Cherokee.

IT WAS AS COLD AS the glacial plains of Algor.

Bram Starbuck rubbed his bare arms briskly with his numbed hands, trying to get the frozen human blood circulating in his veins.

Wherever he was, he'd definitely plotted the coordinates wrong. Because if this was indeed Venice, California, someone in the archival agency had played a Plutonian practical joke by exchanging holotapes. As for proper clothing, for some unfathomable reason, he found himself clad in nothing but a pair of brief white trousers that left his chest, arms, and most of his legs bare.

Damn it to Hadean, despite all reason, regardless of all the years he'd dedicated to planning this mission, somehow, he must have seriously miscalculated.

Starbuck knew that the entire Sarnian scientific community thought him crazy for asking why propelled vehicles must be the only way to bridge the gap between solar systems. Why couldn't it be that physics, not technology, held the ultimate answer to space travel?

After all, Starbuck had pointed out at the annual meeting of interplanetary astrophysicists, any first-level Sarnian was perfectly capable of sending thoughts for hundreds, thousands, of junctures.

By the fourth level, the average Sarnian could send those same thoughts in three-dimensional holographic form. And by the time a Sarnian reached the eighth level of maturity, he was able to utilize telekinesis to move around effortlessly beneath the planet dome.

So why couldn't a person, aided by a pocket-size antimatter accelerator device, travel through the galaxies in an astral or ethereal body?

Why couldn't the component atoms that made up Bram Starbuck be taken apart, transported through space, utilizing the theory of quantum electrodynamics, and be put back together when they'd reached their destination? Indeed, why couldn't they be rearranged to resemble some entirely different life-form?

Despite continued opposition from first the scientific community, and then, when his heretical views became more widely known, from the Sarnian ruling council itself, Starbuck had steadfastly refused to abandon his theory.

Displaying a dogged tenacity and drive that was considered, in his secular society of intellects, to be unseemly, he threw himself into his work.

Such inappropriate behavior resulted in his dismissal from his much sought-after position as head of the space council. Although the outcome had not been a surprise, Starbuck had never expected his peers— those very same scientists who'd once proclaimed him to be one of the most brilliant males on the planet—to shun him.

But they had.

And after he'd published his treatise asking what was wrong with rewriting the laws of physics if they didn't do what you wanted them to, rumors suggesting that lower-class Janurian warrior blood had somehow slipped into his family's gene pool—a gene pool already compromised by Xanthus Valderian's marriage to a terran—had begun to circulate.

Starbuck was accustomed to having his parentage held against him. And all his life, first as a student, then a teacher at the Science Institute, he'd worked overtime to prove himself a true Sarnian.

But, although he'd always done his best to adhere to the Sarnian way, not once, in all his thirty years, had he ever considered denying his humanness.

To do so would have been to deny his mother, and since every Sarnian child was brought up to respect and revere his elders, such behavior would have been totally without reason.

Starbuck also knew intuitively that such denial would have pained him in some intrinsic way he could not quite understand.

Still, the rumors tarnished his family's name and endangered his sister's already tenuous position at the institute.

Although Starbuck didn't give a freebooter's damn what anyone thought of him, he was furious at those who couldn't find anything better to do with their time than to criticize Julianna for her brother's actions.

Cursing violently, evoking the names of ancient, forgotten feudal gods long removed from the official Sarnian calendar, Starbuck forged his way through the driving snow, teeth chattering violently, near-naked body turning to ice.

There were times, and this was definitely one of them, when he almost wished he'd taken his parents' advice and become a twelfth-level Sage, like his father, grandfather and every one of his other male relatives before him, all the way back to Flavian Valderian—one of the original Ancient Ones.

"Well, it's too late now," Starbuck muttered, wondering how long he could last in such hyperborean conditions.

Having chosen California as his destination, he hadn't paid proper attention to the ways terrans adapted to their planet's more frigid climes. Such behavior had been shortsighted, unreasonably careless, not to mention potentially dangerous.

It had also been undeniably human.

The deep-seated stubbornness that had caused him so much grief on his home planet rose to assert itself, keeping his feet doggedly moving forward.

He passed what he suspected was, in warmer seasons, a brook. Now it was a sparkling, shimmering sheet of ice. Water froze on Earth at zero degrees centigrade, Starbuck remembered. Starbuck didn't need a

thermoscan to know that the frigid winter air surrounding him was a great deal colder than that.

Unfortunately, his body—like that of his terran
mother—was seven-tenths water. Did this mean that
he was destined to end up crystallized, frozen in place
like this glistening stilled creek?

No. This couldn't be his fate, Starbuck told himself
over and over again. His labored breath was a wavering white ghost in front of him, freezing on his face.

His last thought, as first his limbs, and then his mind
went numb, was that he'd be damned if he'd die before
proving that he'd been right.

2

THE SNOW BLEW against the windshield, piling up almost faster than the wipers could sweep it away. Drifts blew across the roadway; county snowplows had made high walls of snow along the shoulder. It was dusk, that suspended time between day and night when the world turned a deep purple.

Charity sat hunkered over the steering wheel, peering through the swirling white curtain when she suddenly saw something or someone lying in the center of the road.

Slamming on the brakes, she skidded sideways, missing the snow-covered object by inches. Her heart pounding, she jumped from the Jeep and raced toward what she could now see was a man.

He was unconscious, and nearly naked. Wondering what had happened to cause him to be out here in the middle of nowhere, wearing only a pair of white shorts, she took his pulse, frightened when she found it dangerously weak.

"Hey!"

She ran her hands over his body, feeling for broken bones. Then she checked out his hands and feet and ears, searching for any dead white tissue that would indicate frozen skin.

When she didn't find any, she began briskly rubbing his arms, his face, his outstretched legs. Ice crystals coated his dark hair and eyebrows. Although he looked vaguely familiar, Charity couldn't place him.

Pressing both her gloved hands against his tanned chest, she began to administer CPR, breathing and pushing, breathing and pushing, praying all the time.

Starbuck felt the sweet warmth against his lips first. Then the hard, rhythmic pounding against his chest.

"That's it," Charity shouted when his rigid chest began to rise and fall of its own accord. "You're doing it! You're breathing. Come on, don't give up now. Keep going."

Starbuck read her mind and discovered that she was frightened. The idea that she could care so deeply for another of her kind, one that was a total stranger to her, was something he'd have to think about, later, when he was no longer hovering on the dark abyss of human death.

As she continued to pound painfully but surprisingly effectively on his chest, shouting at him all the while, Starbuck decided with a detached sense of wonder that she was every bit as stubborn as he.

He wondered if such a discordant personality trait made her an outsider, too. The idea that two individuals from such dissimilar planets might have something intrinsically in common was pleasing.

The stranger's breathing was shallow, but steady. She placed her cheek against his chest, rewarded by a reasonably strong heartbeat.

"I can't lift you by myself," Charity complained. "And I certainly can't leave you here to freeze to death. So, you're going to have to help me."

Starbuck opened his eyes and found himself looking straight into hers.

"Help you?"

Since his mother had long ago abandoned her native tongue, Starbuck had been forced to practice his Earth dialect from Julianna's audio disks. Hoping that his accent was appropriate for wherever this was he'd landed, he was relieved when she seemed to find nothing wrong with his speech.

"We have to get you to the truck." Her voice had a much more melodic quality than the computerized tones he'd worked with. "Do you think you can stand up?"

"Of course."

Just because he was no longer on Sarnia, Starbuck had no intention of abandoning aeons of scientific dogma proclaiming the female of the species to be the frailer sex.

Having this Earth woman discover him half-dead was bad enough; to continue to display weakness in front of a female would be a shame he'd never live down. Shaking off her touch, he pushed himself to his feet with a sudden burst of energy.

Stars swam in front of his eyes, his legs trembled. Charity caught him in midsway.

"That's what you get for trying to be Superman," she muttered, putting her arm around his waist to steady him. "Take a few deep breaths. It'll help you get your land legs back."

It crossed Starbuck's whirling mind that she was surprisingly strong for someone of her small stature. The top of her head barely reached his shoulder.

"My land legs?"

"Just an expression," she answered in unison with the ecumenical translator embedded in his middle ear. "Feeling better?"

Amazingly, the deep breathing had helped, immediately clearing his head like a whiff of straight paradoxygen.

"Yes. Thank you," he said with formal politeness drilled into him from the cradle.

She glanced around into the swirling white snow. "Are you all alone?"

"Yes." He wondered what she'd say if he told her precisely how alone he was at this moment.

"You're shaking badly." Her eyes were filled with concern. "Let's get you warmed up. Then you can tell me what happened." Her ground machine appeared to be an older model than those pictured on the archival holotapes. As he made his way gingerly toward it, Starbuck wondered if he'd somehow gone back in time as he passed through space.

Not knowing how to ask such a question without drawing any more undue attention to himself, he decided that explanations could come later.

"Fortunately, I always keep blankets in the Jeep," she told him with a surprising amount of cheer, considering that her own thick lashes were covered with icy white frost.

He climbed into her machine, as she indicated, then sat passively as she wrapped the thick red blanket about his frozen body. He felt light-headed, his hands and feet were numb and the rest of him felt unreasonably clumsy. Starbuck wondered if terrans ever became accustomed to such ungainly corporality.

"There you are." She tucked him in as if he were a child, shut the passenger door of the Jeep, went around the front and climbed into the driver's seat. "What's your name?"

"Starbuck," he told her. Stars were dancing in front of his eyes. Starbuck tried to blink them away and failed. "Bram Starbuck."

That said, he surrendered to the whirling darkness.

"Oh, hell."

Charity cursed under her breath as he crumpled onto the bench seat, his dark head landing in her lap. Reaching over him, she picked up the radio microphone and pressed a button.

"Castle Mountain to Evac Eagle One, Castle Mountain to Evac Eagle One. Do you copy, Eagle One?"

There was a crackling static, then, "Ayuh, I copy ya, Castle Mountain. What's the problem?"

"I've got a patient for you," she said.

"An emergency?"

"Yes. Exposure, possible hypothermia. He's a male, approximately six foot, one hundred sixty pounds." She didn't add that the weight was very attractively distributed on his deeply tanned masculine frame. "Age, around thirty. I found him lying out in the snow."

"How're his vitals?"

"His pulse was thready, but his heartbeat's reasonably strong."

"Conscious?"

"He wasn't when I found him a few minutes ago, then he was, but now he's passed out again."

"Trauma? Broken bones, anything like that?"

"Not that I could tell, but I told you, his pulse isn't as strong as it should be."

"Frostbite?"

"None that I could see. But I've only had paramedic training," she said. "This man needs to be checked out by a physician. And Doc Merryman is in Bangor visiting his daughter."

"Ayuh, I heard his girl had a baby. Boy or girl?"

"A girl. Eight pounds six ounces. What about my patient, Eagle One?"

"Sorry, Castle Mountain," the disembodied voice said over the crackling static, "but it's a no-go."

"What?"

"There's a blizzard blowin'. I can't send out a chopper until the weather clears, Charity."

"I know," she said on a long drawn-out sigh as she glared at the driving snow that had been making her life increasingly difficult.

"But what am I supposed to do with him? The damn ferry's not running because of choppy water."

"Get 'im somewhere dry and warm and cover 'im up to keep 'im from losin' any more body heat."

"I've already done that. I've got him in the Jeep right now, wrapped in a blanket and the heater's going full blast."

"See? Ya don't need me at all."

"Mac—" Charity began warningly.

Just because Joe MacGregor had been her father's best friend and had known her all her life, he thought that gave him the right to tease her the same way he had when he found her sitting on the end of his dock, crying over the two front teeth she'd had the bad timing to lose the day of her first-grade class pictures.

"Sorry," he said. "The thing ta do is keep 'im warm. Since ya can't stay in the Jeep all night, you'd bettuh take him to jail. Or back to your place."

Her place was closer. "Then what?"

"Didn't they teach ya about hypothermia in California?"

"They brushed over it in the police academy, but there's not much need for it on the beach," she countered. "Want to compare notes on heat stroke, sunburn or near drowning?"

"You in a rotten mood today, ain't ya, Charity Prescott?"

"You wouldn't be at your best, either, if you'd had the day I've had," she grumbled.

"Ayuh. We heard about your little green men."

"There weren't any little green men. So, if you don't mind, I'd like to get home before my patient and I get carbon monoxide poisoning from sitting in a car with the motor running."

"Take his temperature. At 94 degrees, ya got confusion. At 90, an irregular heartbeat, at 86 muscle strength gives out and the patient gets drowsy, maybe falls unconscious."

"That's where we are now, I think," Charity said, glancing down at the man sprawled on the seat.

"Ayuh. That's what ya said. If he wakes up and can swallow, give him some warm, nonalcoholic drinks."

"No brandy?"

"That's in the movies," he advised drily. "We don't do that in real life."

"Somebody ought to tell all those Saint Bernards, running through the Alps with kegs around their necks," she muttered. "Okay, so I give the guy some tea. Then what?"

"Like I said, keep 'im covered. Don't take a chance on burnin' his skin with heatin' pads or hot-water bottles, don't leave 'im alone and keep checkin' his vital signs. That's about all ya can do for now."

"Okay. I think I can handle that."

"Who ya got there, by the way?"

"Although he looks vaguely familiar, I can't place him. He's obviously from off island."

"Well, let me know how he's doing. If this damn storm ever blows over, and you still need an Evac, I'll fly to Castle Mountain myself."

"Thanks, Mac."

"Oh, and one more thing."

"What's that?"

"They did teach ya CPR at that California police academy, didn't they?"

"Yes, but—"

"Good. Keep a real close eye on those vitals, Charity. 'Cause if your patient's temperature drops to seventy-seven degrees, ya can expect cardiac arrest. Then death."

She'd seen bodies before, but never one that she'd been personally responsible for. "Don't worry, Mac," she vowed. "I didn't go to the trouble of saving him to have him die on me."

"Ayuh. You're a good gurl, Charity. Your pa'd be right proud of ya." It was the same thing he'd told her when she'd baited her own fishing hook the summer she turned seven. "Good luck."

"Thanks. I think I'm going to need all I can get. Castle Mountain over and out."

She released the button on the radio and looked down at him. "Okay, buster. Let's get you home. And if you even dare try to have a heart attack, I swear I'll toss you in a cell and throw away the key."

When she pushed him off her lap, Starbuck stirred. It took an effort, but he managed to open his eyes. "A cell?"

"Oh, good, you're awake." Her relief was so palpable that Starbuck felt as if he could reach out and touch it. "Don't worry," she assured him. "I'm taking you home with me. You're going to be fine."

She patted his arm reassuringly. Then, shifting the Jeep into gear, she resumed driving.

"How far is it to your home?" Starbuck asked, checking for the accelerator he'd slipped into his pocket at the last minute. Stored warmth radiated from its core.

"It's only about five more miles. We should be there in about fifteen, twenty minutes. I'd go faster, but I don't dare, with all the ice on the road."

Twenty minutes to go a mere five miles! Starbuck shook his head in mute disbelief. Any halfway respectable eighth-level Sarnian could make the trip in less than half a zillisecond.

Reminding himself that he had come to Earth to learn, not to judge, Starbuck conceded that there was one thing about this planet that was far superior to anything on Sarnia.

And that was the marvelously sweet scent emanating from the woman. If all Earthlings smelled like this, Starbuck decided, it would certainly make up for a great many of the planet's other failings.

With that intriguing thought in mind, he passed out again.

CHARITY WAS RELIEVED when he roused long enough to help her lead him into the house. To her surprise, he actually jumped when an orange ball of fur suddenly blocked their path, its howling demand sharp and strident.

"Don't worry," Charity assured him. "It's only Spenser."

"Spenser?"

"My cat. I named him after the detective in all those Parker novels," she explained at his blank look. "And I'm sorry if he frightened you. He's just reminding me that dinner's late." When she reached down and patted the cat's head, it began to purr. The sound reminded Starbuck of a small motor.

"Try to be patient," she advised the cat. "I'm told it's a virtue."

"You own this animal?" Starbuck asked incredulously. He tried to remember the last time he'd seen any animal inside a home and came up blank.

"Obviously you don't know much about cats," Charity said. "*You* don't own them. *They* own you."

Eyeing the animal with distrust and trying his best not to cringe, Starbuck realized that this creature must be the woman's pet. On Sarnia, pets—considered an unnecessary nuisance—had become extinct several hundred solar revolutions ago.

As docile as a kitten, and, she could tell, every bit as weak, he allowed her to lead him to bed before drifting off again.

This had originally been her parents' home. She and Dylan had been born in that bed. And now the cozy cedar house—and the wide antique bed—was hers. On those rare occasions when her brother escaped the lab, Dylan slept in the upstairs loft.

The scant amount of clothing her guest was wearing had nearly dried from the heater in the car. Deciding against stripping him completely naked, Charity piled every quilt she could find in the house over the top of his supine body, then lit a fire in the bedroom fireplace for good measure.

She located a thermometer in the bathroom medicine cabinet, managed to slip it between his lips and under his slack tongue, and after three impatient minutes was relieved to find that his temperature was hovering right around ninety-two degrees.

"Not good," she said as she checked his pulse and found it stronger than when she'd first discovered him lying in that snowdrift. "But better."

After assuring herself that he wouldn't die in the next two minutes, she finally took off her coat and went back into the kitchen, where she served up a can of cat food. Growling happily, Spenser signaled absolute bliss with the chopped chicken livers.

That little domestic chore taken care of, Charity went into the living room and opened the cupboard where her brother had stashed a bottle of cognac last Christmas.

On the table next to the cupboard, the red light was flashing on her answering machine. Knowing intuitively who it was, Charity rewound the tape, listening to the message as she took off her police revolver, placed it on a nearby table and retrieved the liquor.

"Hey, sis," Dylan's deep voice rang out, "I know you're gonna kill me, but I think I had a breakthrough on my quantum jump theory and I need to stay here and run some programs.

"How about breakfast tomorrow morning instead? I'll pick up some blueberry muffins and bagels and see you about nine. I really am sorry. But I think I'm finally on the right track and I promise to dedicate my Nobel prize to you. Sleep tight, kiddo. And don't let any little green men bite."

"Cute, Dylan," Charity muttered. "Real cute." She'd heard all she wanted to about aliens landing on Castle Mountain.

"Maybe you don't need this," she said to the man sleeping in her bed when she returned to her bedroom carrying the bottle of cognac and a balloon glass. "But I do."

She poured two fingers into the glass, reconsidered and added a splash more.

She went into the adjoining bathroom and changed from her uniform into a bulky wool sweater and a pair of corduroy jeans. Then, pulling the rocker her Grandfather Prescott had made for the birth of her sister Faith up to the bed, Charity sipped the cognac as she rocked slowly, all the time keeping a steady, uneasy eye on her patient.

Having finished his dinner, Spenser joined Charity in the bedroom, leaping onto the bed with feline grace, where he settled down for the night, nestled against the stranger.

Charity's vigilance was rewarded when sometime in the middle of the long weary night, his temperature approached normal and his breathing became deep and steady. She pressed her fingers against his dark neck and felt the strong beat of his blood.

"I think you're going to make it," she decided, touching his forehead as she had been doing for hours. "No, I take that back, you're definitely going to make it."

She stretched, rubbing the small of her back as she settled in the rocking chair. She was suddenly exhausted. Her eyes drifted closed.

Charity didn't know how long she slept, but the room was still dark when she jerked suddenly awake. Thinking perhaps her patient had called out, she checked him, only to find him still dead to the world.

She was standing over him, the back of her hand against his forehead, when she thought, against all reason, that she heard a sound in the other room.

She stood absolutely still, drew in a soft breath and concentrated.

Nothing. Then, a soft, recognizable click. The sound was that of her brother's portable computer being switched off.

"Dylan?" Her voice, little more than a whisper, sounded like a shout in the stilled hush of the room. Her patient, murmuring inarticulately in his sleep, rolled over.

"Dylan," she repeated, "is that you?" A strange uneasiness skimmed beneath her skin. The sight of Spenser's suddenly arched back and erect, bristle-brush tail did nothing to calm.

The cat hissed. Charity's breath quickened as she crossed the room and made her way silently, carefully, down the hallway.

The rest of the house was as dark and silent as a tomb.

"Damn it, Dylan," she said as she flicked the switch for the overhead light in the living room. Nothing happened. "This isn't funny."

Making her way carefully across the room, she found the drawer where she kept the flashlight. The batteries were low, the light a faint, stuttering yellow beam, but as she swept it around the room, she could see no one there.

With Spenser weaving through her legs, the cat's bushy tail twitching nervously, Charity made her way over to the old, scarred pine desk that had been her grandfather's and put her hand atop the computer monitor. It was warm.

Which was, of course, absurd. She was obviously all alone in the house. Except for her patient. And he hadn't moved.

"You're going as crazy as the rest of the town," she muttered. Next she'd be seeing little green men raiding her refrigerator.

Still, experience had taught her never to disregard her intuition. Picking up the revolver she'd left on the table just inside the door, Charity began to make a careful check of the doors and windows.

IMAGES FLICKERED on the far reaches of Starbuck's consciousness. Something treacherous was lurking in the darkness, something as deadly as a Janurian pit viper. *She's in danger,* some distant voice warned him. *You must save her.*

Who? From what? Starbuck tossed and turned, struggling to rise above the fog. He tried to lift his eyelids and found, to his frustration, that they'd turned to stone.

"Must rescue her," he mumbled. "Danger."

His hands curled into fists at his side, and with a mighty groan he attempted to rise from whatever bonds were holding him in check. But the effort proved too much and he sank once more back into the dark mists.

THE LOCK ON THE FRONT DOOR was bolted, just as she'd left it. Charity checked the back door and all the windows, which also proved to be locked.

The house was totally secured. If an intruder had gotten in, he would have had to come down the chimney, which, considering the fact that the fire had died down, he possibly could have done. But there was absolutely no way he could have escaped the same way. Unless he was Spiderman. Or Santa Claus.

As for the sudden lack of electricity, that was commonplace on the island during storms. Which was why Dylan had invented a self-operating battery to run his computer.

So, the obvious, only rational answer was that her imagination had simply gotten the best of her. Reminding herself to ask Dylan about solar flares when he showed up with his muffins in the morning, she returned to the bedroom. Spenser followed, leaping onto the bed and, after pawing at the quilts, settling back down with one last warning hiss.

Something had changed.

Her house, always pleasantly cozy, was now strangely alien. As Charity rocked in the chair, the revolver in her lap, her unease grew.

3

CHARITY REMAINED on edge for a very long time. She was filled with an impending sense of awareness mingled with uncharacteristic restlessness and a dark sense of foreboding.

It was only her imagination, she assured herself over and over again as she rocked slowly and continued to observe the man sprawled in the center of her bed. She was only responding to a long, nerve-racking day.

Eventually the events of that day began to catch up with her and her eyelids became heavier and heavier. Unfortunately, the maple rocking chair, while comfortable for short periods, had not been designed for sleep.

She tried borrowing one of her patient's quilts and lying on the pine plank floor beside the bed, but the braided rug and quilt were not enough to keep her from becoming chilled by the cold floor.

There was always the sofa in the other room. But then Joe MacGregor's warning about not leaving her patient alone flashed through her mind. And although she didn't want to admit it, something about the living room made her feel uneasy. Besides, without heat it would soon be freezing in there and she simply wasn't up to building another fire.

"For heaven's sake," she complained, "it's your bed. And it's not as if you're wearing some filmy negligee." She was still wearing the jeans and heavy wool sweater she'd changed into after work, along with a pair of heavy wool ski socks. "Besides, the man's unconscious. What can he do?"

And even if he was capable of trying any funny stuff, she reminded herself that she was, after all, a detective who'd been awarded a commendation for her undercover work. If she could handle the big-city bad guys, she was certainly safe from one near-frozen male who kept passing out on her.

Charity wrapped her mother's quilt tightly around herself, then before she could change her mind, she pushed the cat aside and lay down beside him.

She was asleep the instant her head hit the down pillow.

STARBUCK WAS HAVING the sweetest dream. He was somewhere in Stanza Five, on one of the more hospitable planets, Veneitan, perhaps, lying in a bed of fragrant flowers.

A woman, warm and soft, was wrapped around him, her lips pressed against his throat. Her hair, cut in a sleek, head-hugging cap, was the color of the Sarnian moon, all burnished copper and bronze. He brushed his cheek against the glowing fragrant strands, finding them as silky as woven milkplant.

It had been a very long time since he'd been with a woman. Unfortunately, his work on the quantum accelerator had precluded sufficient time for pleasure.

But now, as he slipped his hand beneath the hem of her tunic, ran his fingers lazily up the delicate bones of her spine and was rewarded by her soft, yielding sigh, Starbuck decided he'd been a Haldon-headed idiot not to make time.

It was only a matter of setting priorities, he told himself, enjoying the feel of her warm flesh against his palm. Or, as Sela was constantly saying, of utilizing proper time management.

Sela was renowned throughout the galaxy for her time-management seminars. The woman was an expert at setting up schedules, organizing her day—her entire life, for that matter—into a series of color-coded time blocks that flashed and buzzed continually on her wrist computer.

Sweet Valhalla, how he'd hated that trigging computer! Especially when he wanted to linger with its owner and the damn thing kept clicking away the time, a digital stopwatch dictating his performance.

Still, he had to admit that Sela was efficient at fitting myriad activities into a single solar period. Perhaps it was time to acknowledge that her criticism of him had merit and ask her to organize him.

If it gave them more time to lie together like this, it would be worth listening to her disparaging comments.

Conveniently forgetting that Sela had coldly broken their bond promise after he'd lost his prestigious position at the institute, Starbuck vowed to turn over a new leaf.

He drew her closer. He pressed his lips against her temple. Her breathing quickened.

"Ah," he sighed. "You're so soft. So warm."

He continued stroking her, enjoying the quiet, inarticulate sounds of pleasure that were a distinct contrast to his bondmate's usual prickly attitude toward anything physical.

"I want to make love to you, Sela. So very much."

It was when his hand moved to her chest that the dream began to waver.

Her breast—covered by a soft fabric that reminded him of the webs spun by the spiders on Centurian—fit into his hand so perfectly that it might have been designed with him in mind.

But how could that be? As she was always so quick to point out, Sela was a perfect Sarnian female.

A superb product of genetic engineering, the woman he'd been promised to at age seven was blond, blue-eyed and slender as a Genetian reed. Since the only logical reason for breasts was to feed a child, Sarnian women—who had utilized surrogates for the unpleasant task of childbearing for the past two centuries—no longer possessed them.

His numbed mind worked through the problem with the lumbering mental speed of a Janurian third-grader:

Sela was a perfect Sarnian.

Sarnian women were all flat chested.

The woman in his arms possessed exquisite breasts.

Therefore, utilizing the most basic deductive reasoning, this woman was not only not Sarnian, she was not Sela.

The logic was flawless.

There was only one problem.

Who the blazing Hadean was she?

CHARITY'S SUN-DRENCHED beach fantasy of the day before had given way to a dream of an isolated ski lodge, somewhere high in the Alps. She'd spent the day schussing the steep, powdery runs with a French count who possessed more titles, charm and money than any one man had a right to.

She knew, from the admiration in his flashing dark eyes, that she looked spectacular in her new, outrageously expensive lipstick-red ski outfit. The brilliantly clever design of the outfit somehow managed to maintain its sleek fit while successfully camouflaging the extra ten pounds she was always vowing to shed. That alone made it worth every penny.

After a last exhilarating run, they'd returned to the quaint lodge that resembled a giant cuckoo clock. Inside, they joined the other guests—Rod Stewart, Madonna, Bruce Springsteen and Ted Koppel—for brandy in the lounge.

But rather than enter into the spirited argument about the importance of quantum physics in overcoming hypothermia the others were engaged in, she and her count were content to exchange long, lingering looks.

Outside, an Alpine blizzard raged.

The voices of the others gradually faded, the room grew uncomfortably warm. They could have been the only two people in the world.

Finally, just when she felt in danger of melting from the lambent flame in his sexy bedroom eyes, the count suavely suggested that they retire to his room.

His obedient manservant, clad in red livery reminiscent of a Swiss Guard uniform—had laid a fire in preparation of their return. The valet struck a match to the kindling, gave a low, sweeping bow, then backed out of the room, leaving them alone.

At last. The moment she'd been waiting for all day had arrived.

His devilish jet eyes didn't move from her own adoring ones as he pulled her down onto the white fur rug in front of the fire. He pressed a kiss against her temple. Then slowly, tenderly, he began to undress her, his strong dark hands doing wonderful wicked things to her body.

"Ah, you're so soft," he crooned as his fingers caressed her breast, creating a glow deep inside her. "So warm. I want to make love to you, Sela. So much."

Sela?

Charity's eyes flew open.

She was staring directly into the all-too-familiar eyes of her dream lover. But those unblinking black eyes didn't belong to a French count any more than they'd belonged to that beach boy she'd fantasized about yesterday afternoon.

"Oh, no," she groaned. Covering her face with her hands, Charity prayed for strength. "It's you."

A memory flashed on the view-screen of Starbuck's mind. A vision of white and cold and dark. Other memories returned. Memories of driving through the snow, the scent of flowers blooming in the warmth of her machine.

Starbuck realized that this was the woman who'd brought him in from the storm. Another vision, of her pounding energetically against his chest flashed in his mind's eye.

"I remember thinking—no, knowing—that I was going to die," he said. "And I would have, were it not for you."

His voice was deep and intense, curling around her, slipping beneath her skin. Charity removed her hands from her face and forced herself to meet those dark eyes that had added so much to her fantasies.

"You saved my life," he said.

"Yes. I suppose I did." She glanced down and realized that his hand was actually under her sweater.

"I'm very sorry," he said, pulling it away before she could say a word. "I didn't mean to offend you." He tried giving her a reassuring smile. "I believe I must have been dreaming."

And what a dream it had been! His fingers practically itched with the desire to slip back under that bulky tunic.

"I understand," she said, trying for the same formal tone. "You were very ill. Close to death, I believe. It would make sense that you might be a little delirious." So what was her excuse?

"A logical deduction," Starbuck agreed. "But I'm afraid that I've upset you."

"No." It was a lie, but only a polite white one. "It's just that I'm not accustomed to waking up in bed with a strange man." Untangling her legs from his, she left the bed.

Starbuck knew that the masculine pleasure he'd received from that simple statement was decidedly human. He'd learned from his studies that terran males were accustomed to claiming women for their own in much the same way they claimed their other prized possessions.

In that respect, they were not so different from Sarnian men. The marriage collar worn by Sarnian wives—a collar Julianna swore never to wear—was a much revered tradition. Starbuck wondered if this woman was claimed.

"You're looking better," Charity said, studying him judiciously, trying not to stare at his smoothly muscled chest.

"I'm feeling better," he agreed. "Thanks to you."

"It's my job."

"It was your kindness," he corrected. "And your tenacity. I will be forever in your debt."

"Gracious," Charity managed on a soft rush of breath, "a simple thank-you will be more than sufficient."

Starbuck took her literally. "Thank you," he said with grave formality. "I do not know your name."

"It's Charity. Charity Prescott."

He extended his hand in the manner prescribed by an ancient terran book on manners Julianna had unearthed in the archives. Although the origin of such a custom was not clear, Julianna had thought it had something to do with showing that the hand carried no weapon.

"I am honored to meet you, Charity Prescott. My name is Bram Starbuck."

"Yes." She held out her own hand. "I know. You told me last night. It's good to meet you, too, Mr. Starbuck."

"Please, my friends call me Starbuck."

The impersonal touch should not have made her pulse leap, or her blood warm. But heaven help her, it did. Uneasy, she slipped her right hand free and crossed her arms over her chest. "So, where are you from, Starbuck?"

He said the first Earth city that came to mind, the one that had been his destination. "Venice, California."

"That explains the tan. How long have you lived there?"

"Not long," he hedged. "Why?"

She shrugged. "It's just a coincidence, that's all. I lived in Venice for six years. So, where are you staying?"

"Staying?"

"Where's your motel?"

"I don't know."

She gave him a long, concerned look. "I suppose that means you don't know where the rest of your things are, either, or what you were doing out here in the middle of a Maine island's woods nearly naked."

A memory flashed through his mind—the sound of Julianna shouting something about Maine.

"I'm in Castle Mountain, Maine?"

Frown lines furrowed her smooth brow. "That's right. It's an island, off the coast."

"What's the date?"

Her frown deepened. "January 18."

At least he'd gotten something right. "What year?"

As easily as he could read the morning news disk, Starbuck read the year that had flashed through her mind and realized that he'd miscalculated by nearly two hundred solar revolutions.

It must have been the magnetic field, he decided. Somehow, it had altered time. He'd have to make the necessary adjustments before returning to Sarnia. He certainly wouldn't want to land on his planet during the brutal ozone wars.

"How much do you remember?" Charity asked.

"The last thing I remember, I was at home."

"In Venice."

"That's right. Venice."

Lying was extremely uncommon behavior for a Sarnian. It wasn't that there was any specific moral prohibition, per se, but the Ancient Ones, in the Book of Laws, had correctly pointed out that one lie inevitably led to another until soon the entire situation had become untenable.

Reason was truth, the elders had written. *Truth, reason. All else was irrational.*

Being half human, Starbuck had found hedging the truth, on occasion, under proper circumstance—such as now—was not that irrational a solution.

"Then," he continued, "the next thing I knew, I was walking down the road—"

"In the middle of the worst snowstorm in fifty years." Her frown deepened. "With hardly any clothes on. If you're not completely off your rocker, I'd say you must have received one heck of a knock on the head."

From the way she was looking at him, Starbuck had the strangest feeling she could see inside his head, which was ridiculous, since he knew for a fact that terrans—even those existing in his own time—were too primitive to possess extrasensory perception.

Still, rather than risk her spotting an out-and-out lie, Starbuck opted for not saying anything.

"You probably have temporary amnesia, from the shock of whatever happened," she diagnosed.

"That is logical." Starbuck thought it was time to change the subject before she decided to take him to whatever passed for the authority in these parts. "Do you have a lav?"

"A lav? Oh, the bathroom." Color rose in her cheeks. "It's right in there." She waved her hand toward a door cut into a wall covered with bright yellow flowers. "You'll find an extra toothbrush in the cabinet. You're free to use my razor, so long as you're not one of those horrid, chauvinistic men who complain that women's legs dull the blade.

"Oh, and you'll need some warm clothes to wear until we track down whatever happened to yours."

She walked over to another door, opened it and began pulling things from hangers. "Dylan, my brother, spends a lot of time here, and lucky for you, you're just about the same size."

When she turned around, he was standing beside the bed, clad only in shorts, looking far too virile for a man who'd been hovering on the brink of death only a few hours earlier.

His shoulders were wide and the mahogany-hued skin of his chest was drawn tautly over sleek, smooth muscles. He must work out, Charity considered. There was not an ounce of excess flesh on his body. His broad shoulders and chest tapered down to a narrow waist and hips. His stomach was as flat as her Grandmother Prescott's old washboard and—

Oh, Lord.

She was obviously not the only one suffering lingering arousal from a sensual dream.

Drawing in a deep breath, Charity dragged her eyes down a few vital inches to his legs. They were long, the muscles of his thighs and calves well-defined, as if he might be a runner.

Lifting her gaze, she found him watching her with unblinking interest. Humiliated at having been caught blatantly staring, Charity dumped the pile of clothes on the mattress, turned and left the room.

It was his fault, Starbuck considered sadly. For some reason he would think about later, her slow, studied appraisal had made his body behave in a most un-Sarnian way.

But why should that cause her such distress? After all, his rebellious body had merely been responding to the human arousal he'd felt momentarily in her own terran mind. So why had she suddenly turned the color of a Sarnian moon and raced out of the room as if all the dogs of Garn were on her heels?

Such behavior was highly illogical.

Unable to solve the equation, Starbuck reminded himself that Julianna had warned him that terrans were a most illogical race. Heaving a weary sigh, he gathered up the clothing and went into the bathroom.

A mirror took up most of one wall. Starbuck stopped in front of it and was both surprised and relieved to see that outwardly, at least, he remained physically unchanged. His relief was short-lived when he was forced to consider the possibility that along with whatever time and location destination miscalculation he'd made, his form-shifting theory had also failed.

Deciding to tackle that problem later, after he'd managed to acquire sufficient scientific data, he glanced around, taking in his surroundings. Flowers bloomed on the walls in this room, as well, delicate purple flowers with dark green leaves.

If all terran homes were like this one, it explained why his mother had spent so much time in her greenhouse. Obviously flowers were more important to a terran than the holotapes had indicated.

A crystal dish shaped like a shell held some dried petals that Starbuck easily recognized. Although the potpourri carried a different, more spicy scent than that Rachel Valderian made from her beloved moonflowers, the idea was the same.

Vowing to create flowers on at least one wall in his mother's home as soon as he returned to Sarnia, Starbuck stripped, stepped into the shower—where more flowers bloomed on the white ceramic tile—and turned the shiny metal knob.

He sucked in a deep breath and jumped back as a blast of frigid water sprayed over him. Having expected a sonic shower, he'd not been prepared for water. And certainly not water that felt as if it came from an Algorian glacier.

Belatedly he noticed the black letters etched into the knobs. Reaching out, he turned toward the *H*, rewarded when the water began to warm. Experimenting, he twisted the knob even more, until the streaming flow was as hot as the sulphur geysers on Ontarian.

Glancing around, he found an alcove cut into the tile. In the alcove was a pink rectangle he suspected was a cleansing bar. He wet it, then rubbed it between his palms; the resultant fragrant froth reminded him of his rescuer.

Tilting back his head, Starbuck closed his eyes and reveled in the glorious feel of the hot water pelting his skin, sluicing over his shoulders, running down his legs. Ten minutes later, the small room was engulfed in a cloud of steam and he'd never felt more relaxed in his life.

It crossed his mind that if there were such showers on Sarnia, the pharmaceutical company that made Valdox would go out of business.

He stepped out of the ceramic cubicle and stood there on the fluffy white rug, legs and arms outstretched, waiting. When he realized that no unseen light or warm breeze was going to dry him, that he was actually expected to do it himself, he looked around the room, saw the stack of purple towels—again, flowered!—took one and began rubbing it against his skin.

He opened a metal cabinet and found the toothbrush she'd mentioned, wrapped in cellophane and thankfully labeled or he wouldn't have recognized it.

The toothpaste, too, was labeled. As he spread the blue gel onto the bristles, then scrubbed them over his teeth, Starbuck wondered how the woman maintained such a dazzling smile using such primitive dental care.

That task out of the way, he brushed his wet hair into reasonable order, decided to pass on the treacherous-looking razor, and dressed in her brother's clothing. Then, following an unfamiliar-but-alluring scent down the hallway, he found himself in a warm and cheery room.

The room was a virtual treasure trove of wood products. The walls were covered with warm, rich golden planks that gleamed like a sunrise over Galactia. Interspersed among the planks were dark knots. The floor was wood, as well, but a darker hue than the walls; the planks were narrower and placed at right angles to one another, creating a series of interlocking squares.

The cat he vaguely remembered from last night was lying on a blue-yellow-and-cream-colored rug—created, Starbuck realized upon closer examination, from scraps of bright cloth—in front of the hearth, eyeing him with unblinking yellow eyes.

Walking over to the window—real glass, he realized, pressing his fingers against the panes momentarily—he saw her standing a few meters away from the house, at the edge of a stand of coniferous trees that reached upward toward the sky like shaggy arrows.

It was still snowing, although instead of blowing sideways in gusts, the hexagonal ice crystals were floating down from the slate sky like drifting feathers.

She was wearing that hooded red coat again, a bright splash of crimson against the white snow, gray sky and dark green trees. Her mittened hands were scattering something over the ground.

He watched, intrigued as a flock of birds descended from hidden branches and began snapping up what he recognized to be a variety of seeds and bread crumbs. They were, as birds were throughout his own galaxy, unreasonably greedy.

They chattered loudly, pecking at one another, fighting over the brown and black seeds as if their lives depended on it. Which, Starbuck considered, gazing around at the glistening white world, was undoubtedly true. He had a feeling that the feathered gluttons were dependent on her for survival.

As he was.

He noticed with surprise that she was actually talking back to the flocking birds. Since none of his studies had shown that terrans possessed the ability to speak to the other species on their planet, he was forced to mark this down as yet another irrational aspect of human behavior.

He made a mental note to pass his observation on to Julianna, who had made quite an illustrious career for herself studying alien social behavior. His sister had risen like a comet through the stuffy ranks of the xeno-anthropology department at the Science Institute, overcoming her dual heritage and her gender.

Apparently finished both with the feeding and the conversation, Charity headed back to the house, trudging through the knee-high snow. When she saw him standing in front of the window, she stopped momentarily in her tracks.

Their eyes met through the clear pane of glass.

And the awareness that flashed through Starbuck's mind staggered him.

For that single heart-stopping moment, Bram Starbuck felt every bit as disoriented as he had last night while stumbling blindly around in that frozen white alien world.

4

TARBUCK RECOVERED QUICKLY.

By the time the door opened, he was feigning interest in the fire blazing in the large stone hearth. There had been a fire in his bedroom, too, Starbuck recalled.

Although such method of heating a room was distressingly primitive, not to mention being an almost sacrilegious waste of rare wood, he couldn't deny that the fragrance of the burning log and the way the heat waves radiated against his outstretched hands were most pleasing.

"Well, you definitely look as if you're going to live," Charity greeted him as she entered the kitchen.

"I believe I am. Thank you for letting me use your shower. The hot water was very enjoyable."

"I'll bet it was, after yesterday." She shrugged out of her thick coat and hung it on a hook.

Her trousers were identical to the ones she'd given him. Blue and woven from some soft, pliable fiber. They fit her a great deal better, he decided, taking in the way they hugged her very feminine hips.

She'd changed into a different tunic. This one, Starbuck noticed, was softer in both fabric and hue. It reminded him of a vapor cloud tinged with pink moonlight.

Beneath the fluffy fabric, her breasts were softly rounded. He jammed his hands into the pockets of his trousers so that he couldn't touch her.

Shaking off the odd, disturbing tug at his senses, he said, "Did I hear you correctly? Your name is truly Charity?"

Starbuck remembered that the word meant kindliness and decided that she'd chosen well. Considering the danger a stranger might represent, leaving him for dead probably would have been the more rational thing to do.

"I know." She grinned, flashing him the whitest teeth Starbuck had ever seen. "It's horribly old-fashioned, like a heroine in some nineteenth-century novel. Or worse yet, a chapter from Pilgrim's Progress.

"My sisters are Faith and Hope, which might make you think my mother is old-fashioned, but the truth is that she's always been a thoroughly modern woman.

"Before marrying my father, she danced for Martha Graham's dance company and right now, as we speak, she's down in Tahiti somewhere painting natives like Gauguin."

Starbuck had no idea what she was talking about. He also didn't want her to stop. Her voice reminded him of music; he could listen to it for hours.

"But she did seem to turn distressingly Victorian whenever she named her children. Prudence and Modesty were next on her list, but she ran out of girls.

"Not that she was going to let that stop her. My twin brother was going to be called Loyal until my father put his foot down and claimed the right to name his only son, which was awfully lucky for Dylan, don't you think?"

What he thought was that her eyes were incredible. Looking into them was like looking into two shimmering blue pools.

"That's my brother's name," Charity continued cheerfully. "Dylan. After the poet, not the folksinger."

Small talk was an alien thing to Sarnians. They were far too reserved to engage in idle conversation. Also, because of their highly developed intellect and need for exactitude, they preferred choosing one singularly appropriate word when other species might use two or three less perfect ones.

The terrans who visited his parents' house had always been fairly talkative, as were the Freemasians, that alien group responsible for construction and repair on the planet.

And of course the gregarious shuttlecraft agents from Blarninian were infamous for being able to talk a blue streak when trying to talk you into purchasing a shiny new model of ground transportation, even when your current one was quite sufficient. But even the most loquacious outlanders would have appeared taciturn when compared to Charity Prescott.

Her words were coming at him like pulsars. Starbuck was doing his best to keep up, but even with the ecumenical translator decoder working at full speed, he couldn't comprehend half of what she was talking about.

A slight grinding sound caught his attention. Starbuck glanced over at the wall, where he saw a small replica of a house similar to Charity's. As he watched, a door opened, and a toy bird popped out of the house, chirped a few times in a ridiculously artificial voice, then disappeared behind the door again. Belatedly he realized that the foolish-looking little bird had counted off the hour. What a strange, illogical way to tell the time, Starbuck mused.

"What of your father?" he asked, returning his mind to their conversation. "Where is he?"

"He died a few months ago."

Although it was irrational, since he'd had no way of knowing, Starbuck could have kicked himself for having been responsible for the light fading from her remarkable blue eyes.

"I'm sorry," he said quietly.

"So I am. He was a wonderful man. Everyone loved him."

"My father was most revered, also," Starbuck heard himself saying.

"Oh? Is he—"

"He died as well," Starbuck said. "Last year. I am just coming to grips with the idea that he's gone."

Death on Sarnia was not a time for grief. It was, Starbuck had always been taught, merely the natural order of things. The old giving way to the new.

However, when his father had ceased to exist during the last solar revolution, Starbuck had experienced a startling deep feeling of pain and an even stronger sense of loss that were distressingly human.

"Grieving takes its own time," Charity agreed. "How is your mother taking it?"

"She doesn't say very much, but I suspect that she is still grieving because she has immersed herself in her work a great deal more than she did when Father was alive."

"That's the same thing my mother did. The day after the funeral she was off to Tahiti. Some people might consider that uncaring of her, but both Dylan and I know it's because she cared so much about Daddy that she couldn't stay here."

She shook her head slightly, as if to shake off painful memories. She walked over to a clear glass container, poured a dark liquid into a mug, causing fragrant steam to rise.

"Would you like some coffee?"

Having no idea what he was agreeing to, but anxious to please, Starbuck said, "Yes, thank you."

He curled his fingers around the container she was holding out toward him, took a tentative sip and found, to his surprised pleasure, that it tasted rather like the caffoid tablet he chewed each morning. But much, much better.

And a decided improvement over the herbal teas his house-droid prepared. Teas that tasted like chlorophyll.

"This tastes wonderful."

Charity rewarded him with a smile. "What a nice thing to say. Unfortunately, black coffee is the apex of my culinary skills. Of course, even that took a lot of practice. In fact, on my first night working the graveyard shift at the Venice Police Department—oh, no!" She slammed her mug down on the counter. "I forgot all about it," she moaned.

Pulling on a pair of thick, oversized blue mitts that looked like the gloves worn by members of the confederation fleet's decontamination team, she lifted a dark pan from a white cabinet.

"Oh, damn. It's ruined."

He studied the charred contents of the pan thoughtfully. "So it seems," he agreed. "May I ask what it was?"

"Grandmother Prescott's pot roast." Charity's shoulders slumped. "It was supposed to cook for ten and a half hours at two hundred degrees."

He studied the arcane dial he took to be a thermo-
stat. "The temperature is set at two hundred degrees."

"But I was supposed to take it out last night. Dylan
was coming to dinner."

"It was my fault," he offered in an attempt to soothe
the lines etching her smooth brow. "You were distracted."

"No, it's not your fault."

She dragged her hand through short sleek hair that
Starbuck mentally compared to the gleaming hue of the
copper silicate ore mined on the planet Orionas.

"I'm just a lousy cook," she muttered.

Her obvious distress tugged at something elemental
inside Starbuck. "But you make very good coffee. I believe you were telling me about when you first learned
to make it so well," he reminded her, wanting irrationally to make her smile again.

He was partially successful. Although her faint smile
lacked the dazzle of her earlier grin, Starbuck found it
no less appealing.

"You're just trying to get my mind off my failure."

"Yes," he responded with absolute Sarnian honesty.
"I am."

She looked at him curiously for a moment, then
shrugged. "Well, you have to understand that I really
wanted to fit in, to become part of the squad."

"Highly understandable," he agreed. "Teamwork is
often preferable to individual effort."

She gave him another brief, inquisitive glance. "Yes.
Well, anyway, I offered to make coffee for the men,
which I realize would make most feminists, my sister
Hope and my mother included, hit the roof, but it
seemed like a good idea at the time."

Her sister and mother sounded like Julianna, who was constantly lecturing about female rights. Although Starbuck could understand his sister's frustration, and he could even admit that she was the one woman who was probably intellectually equal to a male, he could not, in good conscience, agree with her desire to abolish the rigid structure of what was a very efficiently run patriarchal society.

"One taste and the desk sergeant threatened to lock me up and throw away the key if I ever poisoned his police force again."

"You poisoned the police?"

Although the constabulary on Sarnia were needed solely to keep the immigrants from other planets in line, every Sarnian possessed a deep-seated respect for The Law.

"Not really," Charity assured him. "I was only speaking figuratively. But I did decide right then and there not to put the sergeant to the test.

"So, I called my sister Faith and got her recipe for coffee, and after working my way through nearly an entire can of beans, I finally got it right.

"Faith makes perfect coffee, but then, she always does everything perfectly," Charity said without rancor. "I got the recipe for the pot roast from her. You can bet your Reeboks that Faith never turned a piece of chuck roast into shoe leather."

Starbuck couldn't understand her concern about the pot roast. It was obviously ruined. So why dwell on something she could not change?

This woman was quite possibly the most illogical being—other than the gossamer-winged flitterflys on Evian 4—he'd ever come across. But appealing, in an irrational sort of way, Starbuck decided.

"You were a clerk in this police force?"

From the way her soft curves molded the trousers and pink tunic, Starbuck had the feeling that she'd look pleasingly attractive in the thigh-high dark blue tunics worn by the Sarnian police clerks.

"I was a cop," Charity corrected.

"A what?"

"A cop," she repeated.

In his ear, the ecumenical translator informed him the unfamiliar word was a colloquialism for a law-enforcement officer.

"Actually," Charity said with discernible pride, "I'd made detective before I quit to move back here."

"You were a policeman?" He didn't even try to conceal his disbelief.

She sighed and shot him a quick look. "Detective third-class. And now I'm the police chief of Castle Mountain, which truthfully isn't that big a deal since the entire force consists of a part-time deputy, Andy Mayfair, and me."

"A police chief," he murmured, trying to understand what type of skewed logic could allow a female—and a small female at that—to work at such a dangerous post.

"That's right." Her eyes narrowed and red warning flags waved in her cheeks. "Do you have a problem with that?"

The ecumenical translator had never failed him. Logic told him that it was operating properly. Still, Starbuck could not believe he was understanding her correctly.

"What were your duties in Venice? When you were a detective, third-class?"

"I worked in the rape and domestic violence section and spent a month undercover, which resulted in the arrest and conviction of the Surfer rapist, a serial creep who'd been terrorizing women on the beaches for over a year. Okay?"

"That sounds dangerous." He wondered why her father, who obviously would have been alive at the time, or her bondmate, would permit her to hold such a risky position.

She shrugged. "So's running around in a blizzard in shorts. You might be all the fashion rage on the beaches of Venice, Starbuck, but you were definitely underdressed for Maine."

She frowned. "Speaking of last night's little adventure, we probably should get you to a hospital for a checkup."

"I don't want to go to a hospital."

"I don't really care what you want," she snapped in a way that no properly acquiescent female on Sarnia would ever dare to do.

He folded his arms across the front of the black ski sweater and glared down at her. "And if I refuse?"

She lifted her chin and met his challenging glare head-on. "I wouldn't advise putting me to the test."

Gone was the blithe spirit who'd chattered on like a brightly plumed jabberkeet. In her place was a brisk, take-charge law-enforcement official who could have held her own with any uniformed, stun-pulsar-carrying policeman on Sarnia.

"But you're in luck," she said. "For now. Because until this snow stops, there's no way I can get you to the mainland."

Her obviously reluctant decision caused a cooling wave of relief to flow through Starbuck. He'd had no

intention of allowing her to take him to the hospital.
What he hadn't determined was how far he was willing
to go to stop her.

"Whatever you say," he said mildly. Charity shot him
a quick, suspicious look.

"We need to unravel the mystery of what happened
to the rest of your clothes," she said. "It's really strange.
We never have muggings here on the island, and theft
is almost unheard of."

The orange flames of the fire were warming the
room. The coffee was spreading through him, soothing his body even as it stimulated his brain.

He was relieved that although his body might be that
of a terran, his mind had remained Sarnian. Ending up
with the undeveloped brain of a terran had been the one
variable that had secretly concerned him.

All the archival data described the residents of Earth
to be a benign, if unpredictable and occasionally violent, race. Which was perfectly explainable when you
considered that the planet itself was still in its adoles-
cence.

Aeons from now, if they could avoid destroying their
world with their careless pollution and unending ter-
ritorial disputes, they would, as his own people had,
evolve to a point that such problems as war and dis-
ease and poverty would be a distant memory. Something to be taught in ancient history classes.

"Oh, my God." Grabbing hold of the back of a chair,
Charity sank onto the rush seat.

Starbuck recognized the name of one of Earth's dei-
ties, but from her startled tone he knew she was not
praying.

"What's wrong?"

She was looking at him, her gaze wide with shock.

"I suddenly realized why you look familiar."

"Why's that?" Starbuck asked with a great deal of trepidation. What if he resembled someone she knew? Someone she disliked?

He had learned from Julianna's disks that Earthlings were an emotional race, and the females were reputed to be especially mercurial during their lunar cycles.

What would he do if she threw him back out into that icy white stuff to fend for himself?

"You're the man in my fantasy."

Her voice, which had remained as strong and steady as catonium during their crisis last night, was now soft and thready.

"I was dreaming about you."

"Dreaming?"

"Well, technically it was a daydream. Right before all the UFO calls."

So he had been seen. Starbuck had hoped that the lights of the aurora borealis would have allowed him to slip in undetected.

"UFO calls?"

"Don't worry about that. We always get a few crank calls during a full moon. I've got a feeling that the solar flares are somehow involved, too," she confided. "But I don't know if there's any scientific data backing me up."

He knew the answer, of course, but decided there was no logical way to reveal it, without also having to explain that the study proving solar flares intensified feelings of excitement and anticipation was still five solar revolutions in the future.

Something clicked in Starbuck's memory banks. "Did you say your brother's name was Dylan Prescott?"

The benchmark study of solar flare arousal, which was still being taught in Sarnian astrophysical psychology classes, had been developed by a scientist named Dylan Prescott.

In fact, Galileo, Copernicus, Newton, Darwin, Einstein, Prescott and Pournelle were the only Earthlings who'd ever earned mention in the Sarnian textbooks.

And even then there were footnotes pointing out that these seven men were not considered representative of their species. They were, the textbook writers had felt it necessary to stress, highly exceptional.

"That's him," Charity said. "Oh, Lord, is that what you're doing here? Have you come to recruit him, too?"

"Recruit him?"

"Every university and think tank in the country—the world, actually—has been after my brother since he was nine. He graduated from medical school at eighteen," she said. "Then he went to M.I.T. and earned his doctorate in physics in two years. That's when things got really crazy.

"After weighing all the offers, he went to work at a famous think tank in Boston, but he didn't stay there very long."

"What happened? Wasn't the work challenging enough?" It would take, Starbuck knew, a great deal to challenge Dylan Prescott's remarkable intellect.

"Dylan would never tell me. All I know is that he left abruptly after an unpleasant disagreement with Harlan Klinghofer, the man who ran the institute. Something about twisting data to falsify results.

"You've no idea how viciously competitive the scientific community can be," she informed Starbuck. "Anyway, after Dylan left Boston, he established his lab out here in the middle of nowhere. It gives him more privacy."

Starbuck knew firsthand exactly how brutal the supposedly lofty, idealistic world of scientific exploration could be.

But his lingering frustration over his dismissal from the Science Institute was overridden by the discovery Dylan Prescott was actually living here, in Castle Mountain, Maine. Starbuck decided that being in proximity to such brilliance more than made up for his arriving in the wrong time.

"I didn't come here to meet your brother."

"Good. Because I'd hate to have to call him and tell him not to come to breakfast because another head-hunter is after him."

"I'm not a headhunter." Starbuck had no idea what such a man might be, but considering the propensity for violence of this planet's inhabitants, he didn't want to dwell on the possibilities. Especially not some of the ones currently being provided by the translator.

"Maybe you were working at the lab with Dylan," Charity suggested. "That might explain why you were dressed so weird."

In quest of a comfortable lap, the cat left the warmth of the fire and leaped onto Starbuck's thighs, draping itself bonelessly over him.

"Just push him down," Charity advised.

"He's fine," Starbuck said, not quite truthfully. He was still decidedly uncomfortable with the idea of bringing wild creatures into the house. "Why would my mode of dress make you think I was working in your brother's laboratory?"

"Well, I certainly don't want to hurt your feelings, in case you are working at the lab, but most of the people

I've met from out there are definitely living in their own little worlds."

Having devoted the past six years of his life to this particular project, Starbuck could identify with that. "Including your brother? Is he working in his own little world?"

She laughed at that, a soft, musical sound that Starbuck liked. A lot.

"Oh, Dylan's the worst of the bunch. In fact, my twin brother is so far out in space, he has to have his mail delivered by space shuttle."

Knowing that the first colony of terrans in space was 48.6 years in the future, Starbuck decided she must be speaking figuratively again.

Wanting to know exactly what Dylan Prescott was currently working on but deciding that those questions could wait until later, he brought his mind back to something else Charity had told him.

"You said you dreamed about me," he reminded her. "About a man who looked like me."

"Yes. Well." She sighed. "It's going to sound foolish, but I was sitting at my desk, watching the snow come down—as it has for days—and I was feeling a little sorry for myself, so I began fantasizing about being back on the beach, at Venice. The sun was bright and hot and the sand was warm and you were rubbing coconut oil on me."

Starbuck's first thought was that this explained how he'd gotten his wires crossed. When he'd been scanning minds, searching through the myriad random thoughts for a link to Venice, California, he'd managed to stumble into this woman's romantic fantasy.

His second thought was that perhaps there wasn't anything wrong with his form-shifting theory, after all.

As amazing as the mathematical odds must be against such an occurrence, Charity had been daydreaming of a man who looked like him. That being the case, there had been no reason for his features to change.

His third and most intriguing thought was the idea of spreading oil all over Charity Prescott's body. As Starbuck focused on the appealing mental image forming in her mind, he considered that perhaps his detractors were right about him being a throwback.

"That sounds like a very good fantasy," he said.

"I don't know why I'm telling you all this," she murmured, more to herself than to him. "It must be the solar flares. I'm really going to have to talk to Dylan about how odd everyone, including me, has been behaving lately."

Color that had nothing to do with the frigid air outside the house flooded into Charity's cheeks. What on earth had gotten into her, sharing such an intimate thought with a total stranger?

But he wasn't exactly a stranger, was he? After all, in a strange sort of way, she'd dreamed him up.

"Do you believe in ESP?" Charity asked.

"Of course," Starbuck answered promptly. Finally, he thought with a great deal of relief, a common ground.

"I never did," she admitted. "Except for the sometime twin thing I share with Dylan. But I never accepted the idea of telepathy. Of course part of that probably stems from the fact that I was born and bred in Maine, and Lord knows we're a practical bunch.

"But how do you explain the fact that I was thinking about you at the very same time you needed my help? It's almost as if we're connected, on some strange sort of mental level."

She risked a quick glance at him. "Boy, I really sound like I'm ready for the funny farm, don't I?"

The idiom had not been on Julianna's data disks, but before the translator could sense his unfamiliarity with the colloquialism and decode, Starbuck had gotten the general idea.

"Not at all. There are a great many unsolved mysteries in the universe." But now, thanks to him, intergalactic travel without a spaceship was no longer one of them.

"I suppose so," Charity agreed reluctantly. The idea was still too remarkable, and vaguely disturbing, to accept.

She fell silent, immersed in her own thoughts, thoughts Starbuck could easily read but didn't, deciding that after saving his life, she was entitled to some privacy.

Under normal conditions, Starbuck would never have intruded on another's personal thoughts without first being invited. Such a breach of etiquette was highly un-Sarnian.

He had always struggled to keep his telepathic powers bound in check by a steely control. Sometimes too much control, his terran mother had worried. But despite Starbuck's best intentions, sometimes the reins slipped.

As they had with this woman. Writing such unpremeditated indiscretion off to his near-death experience, Starbuck vowed to maintain stricter control in the future.

The warmth from the fire caused her fragrance to bloom in the room like his mother's hothouse moonflowers.

Starbuck sipped the hot coffee, drank in her alluring scent and decided that although it definitely wasn't California, Castle Mountain, Maine, would do quite nicely, after all.

5

A STRIDENT SOUND from somewhere in the woods shattered the morning silence.

"That'll be Dylan," Charity said.

She stood up, walking over to the window, pushed aside the blue-and-white gingham curtains and peered out into the falling snow. The cat glanced up at her with vague interest, then apparently deciding no food was to be offered, stretched and went back to sleep atop Starbuck's lap.

The sound grew closer. A moment later, two figures, one in bright orange, the other in black, seated astride a black machine that reminded Starbuck of a jetcycle, came to an abrupt stop outside the door.

"Oh, beans."

"What's wrong?"

"He brought Vanessa with him."

"You do not like this Vanessa?" He didn't need to read her mind—lines bracketed her rosy lips, furrowed her brow.

"Not really," she admitted with obvious reluctance. "Although to tell you the truth, I don't have any reason not to. She's always been polite to me, and it seems that she honestly likes my brother, but whenever she's in the room I have this gut feeling...." Charity shook her head. "You really are going to think I'm crazy."

If what she said was true, Starbuck would have to agree that it was illogical for Charity Prescott to dislike her brother's female friend. But his own experience had taught him that instinct, while not always rational, was to be trusted.

"I think you care a great deal for your brother," he said.

"I love him," Charity responded. "More than anything. And I honestly want him to settle down with a loving wife and have a houseful of little geniuses."

"But not with Vanessa."

"No. Not with Vanessa." Charity sighed and gave him a crooked smile. "Personally, even allowing for scientific eccentricity, I get bad vibes whenever I'm around her."

"Vibes?"

"You know, vibrations," Charity elaborated. "Feelings. Like intuition."

"I've found that intuition can be a valuable tool."

"Me, too. And I've always had a pretty good sense of people, I mean, sometimes back in California, my work, and even my life depended on it, you know?"

Still having trouble imagining this woman as a law-enforcement officer, Starbuck merely nodded.

"The problem is, that whenever Vanessa's around, my needle just starts going off the Richter scale."

Even as Starbuck struggled to make logic of the statement, she said, "But it really isn't any of my business, is it?"

As if on cue, the kitchen door opened and the pair on the machine burst into the room, bringing with them a stiff gust of icy air.

Dylan Prescott, clad in a bright orange jumpsuit resembling those worn by Sarnian transport pilots, was a great deal taller than his sister, even allowing for the expected differences between male and female. His eyes were a deeper shade of blue.

When he pushed back his hood, his hair, Starbuck noticed, was not the bright copper silicate hue of his sister's, but rather a glistening black that resembled the obsidian mountains of the Sarnian moon Australiana.

The resemblance, Starbuck decided, was in the slant of the cheekbone—although what was delicately formed on Charity was a rugged slash on Dylan—and the full, sensual lips.

"Lord, it's cold enough out there to freeze the—" When he caught sight of Starbuck, Dylan stopped in midsentence.

"Well. Hello." His tone was polite, his intelligent eyes filled with both a curiosity, which Starbuck suspected was second nature, and surprise.

For the second time this morning, Starbuck experienced a very un-Sarnian-like satisfaction to realize that a man in Charity Prescott's house first thing in the morning was not a common sight.

Dylan pulled off his gloves and thrust out a hand. "I'm Dylan Prescott, Charity's brother."

Starbuck brushed the cat off his lap, rose and shook hands. "Bram Starbuck."

"And a dead ringer for Heathcliff," Dylan's companion offered.

She pulled off her gloves, looking at him as if he were a specimen in some laboratory experiment. "I'm Vanessa Reynolds."

Starbuck nodded. "I know."

She arched a delicate brow. "Oh? I hadn't realized my fame was such that my name would have garnered recognition."

"I wouldn't know about that," Starbuck said frankly. "I knew your name because Charity informed me that her brother's companion's name was Vanessa."

"Oh?" Thin lips, outlined in a pale shade that was nearly as white as the snow outside, twitched in something that resembled a smile as Vanessa glanced over at Charity. "And what else has Charity told you about me?"

"You two must be absolutely freezing," Charity said quickly. Too quickly. It was obvious to everyone in the room that she didn't want to continue this particular line of questioning. "Let me pour you both some coffee."

"Charity makes excellent coffee," Starbuck offered.

"I'm sure she does. But I'd prefer herbal tea," Vanessa said, turning to Charity. "If you have it."

"I think I've got some Red Zinger," Charity offered with far less enthusiasm than Starbuck had witnessed from her thus far.

"Perfect." Vanessa flashed a smile at Starbuck. "I prefer not to put artificial stimulants into my body. And caffeine definitely affects my ability to concentrate. Which in my work could be disastrous."

"What is your work?" Starbuck asked politely.

"Genetics."

"Ah. A fascinating field."

Coming from a mixed marriage, Starbuck had always found genetics interesting. Especially since he had inherited a disturbing amount of human traits.

"Then you must work at the laboratory. With Dylan."

"Why, yes. We work together." Vanessa exchanged a glance with Charity's brother that suggested work was not the only thing they had in common. "Well, not exactly together, of course. We're involved in different projects."

Wanting to learn more about Dylan Prescott's current work, he was about to inquire as to the nature of those projects when Dylan said, "How do you know my sister?"

Dylan's face, so open and friendly and curious earlier, had closed up, like a window with black shutters suddenly drawn. There was an energy radiating from him that was in no way hospitable.

"I found Starbuck out on the road yesterday," Charity divulged as she filled a copper kettle with water for Vanessa's tea. "He was unconscious and suffering from hypothermia. Most of his clothes had been stolen, so I lent him some of yours."

"I thought that sweater looked familiar," Dylan agreed. Although his tone was mild, his eyes, as they riveted on Starbuck's, were not. "What are you doing in our neck of the woods, Mr. Starbuck?"

"Please, just Starbuck."

"That's what his friends call him," Charity supplied as she put the kettle on the stove.

"I'm not sure what I'm doing here," Starbuck hedged.

That much was the truth. So far, nothing about this experimental travel had gone as planned and he still had to work out how he was going to get back to Sarnia to the proper time.

"He has amnesia," Charity said helpfully.

"Amnesia." Dylan chewed that over for a minute, appearing openly suspicious. "Interesting."

"It's also a little unsettling," Starbuck said. "And although I'm not sure how I ended up in Castle Mountain, I do know that I'm not a headhunter.

"Although I won't deny that I have heard of you," he tacked on, struggling to maintain some balance between the white lie born of necessity and the Sarnian dictates of honesty and reason.

"Really." Dylan took the mug his sister offered. "Thanks," he murmured, slanting her a distant smile that didn't quite reach his eyes.

He took a sip, continuing to eye Starbuck thoughtfully over the rim of the mug. "If you have amnesia," he said slowly, "how would you know that you're not a headhunter?"

Good question, Starbuck acknowledged. And as highly logical as he would expect from a man with such a scientific mind. "I would know." His tone was strong and sure.

"Amnesia," Vanessa said on a long, heartfelt sigh. "This is so wonderfully romantic. A dark, Heathcliffian hero, stranded in the blizzard, is rescued by our heroine, only to realize, after spending the night together, that he can't remember who he is."

She smiled suggestively at Charity. "I know women who'd kill to be able to live out that particular fantasy. For just one night."

"We didn't spend the night together," Charity flared.

Starbuck wondered if she would exhibit the same passion in bed, then, remembering the way Charity practically melted in his arms this morning, decided that with the right man, she just might.

"At least not the way you mean," she said stiffly, damning the color that flooded into her cheeks.

"Besides, Starbuck remembers his name," Charity pointed out.

"A fugue," Dylan murmured more to himself than to the others.

"A fugue? Like a musical composition?" Charity asked. Accustomed as she was to her brother's thoughts moving from subject to subject with amazing speed and alacrity, she could not connect this latest leap in topic.

"Same pronunciation," Dylan told her. "Different meaning. I was referring to the psychiatric definition in which an amnesiac may leave home and start wandering around, ultimately beginning a new life."

"Do you think that's what happened in Starbuck's case?"

For the first time since he learned of her occupation, Starbuck could envision her as a law-enforcement official. He could practically see the wheels turning inside her head. Indeed, as his mind slipped easily into hers, he realized that she was seriously considering faxing—whatever the hell that was—his picture to other police departments in the area.

"It's possible," Dylan said. "Particularly if he's had an injury to the brain."

"Isn't there something you can do?" Vanessa asked. "Hypnosis? Or drugs?"

"Sodium amytal or sodium pentathol and hypnosis have all been used to help memory," Dylan allowed. "But only if the cause of the amnesia is emotional."

Although Starbuck did not want to be impolite, he was growing extremely irritated by the way they were talking about him as if he weren't even in the room. Or worse, as some potential laboratory experiment.

"I'm certain that my amnesia will be short-lived," he said, his tone more testy than he'd planned. "As you've pointed out, Dr. Prescott, a blow to the head is undoubtedly the cause."

Dylan's brows drew together into a worried frown. "How did you know I was a doctor?"

"I told him," Charity said on an exasperated huff of breath. "I also accused him of having come here to track you down, but he assured me that's not the case. And I believe him."

Her tone implied that the subject was closed. But only for now, Starbuck determined, eyeing the still-interested glint in Dylan Prescott's gaze. Possessing a decidedly un-Sarnian amount of tenacity himself, Starbuck could recognize and appreciate that trait when he saw it in others.

"By the way, Dylan," Charity said, unaware of the look that passed between the two scientists, "next time you decide to have your computer in the brain factory start talking with the one here in the house, I wish you'd give me advance notice. That stunt you pulled last night cost me some much-needed sleep."

"What stunt?"

Charity felt a chill much like the one she'd experienced last night shimmy up her spine. "You didn't plug in to the computer?"

"I didn't need to. I had all the data I needed at the lab." His dark eyes narrowed. "What makes you think I did?"

Charity forced a shrug. "I thought I heard a noise. When I went to check, I could have sworn your monitor was warm. But all the windows and doors were locked, so I suppose I must have simply drifted off and dreamed I heard something." She laughed with forced casualness. "You know my overactive imagination...so, where are those muffins you promised me?"

"Right here." Dylan reached into a backpack. "I also brought some whole wheat bagels—" he pulled out a white container "—and cream cheese."

"Cream cheese," Charity said on a pleased note that Starbuck would have expected from a woman who'd just received the deed to her own diamaziman mine. "You're forgiven for skipping out on dinner."

As he put his packages onto the counter, Dylan glanced over at the charred piece of meat. "Speaking of dinner, it looks as if I lucked out. That's not how I remember Grandmother Prescott's pot roast."

"There was a slight accident," Charity muttered.

"I can see that. When did the fire department leave?"

"In case you haven't noticed, Charity is not the domestic type," Vanessa informed Starbuck needlessly.

Starbuck noticed how Vanessa's comment gave birth to a hot flash of irritation in Charity's eyes. Strangely, and highly illogically, since Charity had openly admitted the same thing about herself, Starbuck felt a similar annoyance.

"It was my fault," he said. "Charity was about to turn off the oven, when I became delirious and distracted her."

"Delirious?" Dylan asked.

"Yes." Starbuck studiously avoided what he knew would be Charity's surprised expression. "I vaguely recall her saying that she had to tend to her dinner and would return shortly, but then this feverlike state came over me and I drifted into a strange, dreamlike world, and when I came out of it much, much later, she was still beside me, soothing me like the lovely angel of mercy she is."

Unable to resist, Starbuck looked at Charity, whose flushed cheeks had nothing to do with the warmth of the kitchen fireplace.

A shared memory of the way they'd awakened in each other's arms shimmered between them, warm and seductive. That memory was immediately followed by mental images of Charity's alleged earlier fantasy, of Starbuck spreading fragrant oil all over Charity Prescott's near-naked body. The fantasy that had brought him to Castle Mountain in the first place.

Starbuck didn't need Sarnian telepathy to know that they were sharing the same thought.

And finally, just when the air in the room seemed filled with heat and smoke, another more recent memory gripped them. They once again saw each other through a pane of glass that had done nothing to temper the emotions that had, for one stunning, frightening moment, joined their minds in perfect, sensual harmony.

"Gracious." Vanessa began fanning herself with her hand. "Has it suddenly gotten extremely hot in here? Or is it me?"

Silence had descended on the room like a curtain. When Dylan's intelligent gaze met his once again, Starbuck felt that he was being thoroughly summed up.

He managed, with effort, to meet that challenging gaze with a bland look of his own, realizing as he did so, that Dylan Prescott's midnight-blue eyes never missed a thing.

"I think," Dylan said finally, shattering the expectant silence, "that I'll go for a walk."

"It's freezing out there," Charity protested. "Besides, you just got here."

"And now I'm going for a walk." He was talking to her, but as he pulled his gloves back on, his eyes didn't leave Starbuck's. "Would you care to join me, Starbuck? I believe I left an old ski parka in the closet."

Starbuck had never been one to turn away from a challenge. "I'd enjoy a short walk," he agreed. "Perhaps it will stimulate my memory."

"Just what I was thinking," Dylan agreed.

THE AIR WAS CRISP and clear and icy. Starbuck breathed shallowly, not wanting to draw too much of the freezing air into his lungs. After his near-death experience yesterday, he was not yet at ease in such frigid climes.

He was not surprised when Charity's brother got right to the point. "All right," Dylan said, stopping in a grove of pine trees not far from the house, "what the hell are you up to?"

"I don't know what you mean," Starbuck said carefully. "If you're referring to my alleged interest in you or your work—"

"I don't give a damn about any interest you might have in me," Dylan said on an explosion of frosty breath. "If you've come here to try and recruit me, you're wasting your time. If you're here to steal my work or try to sabotage it in any way, I'm capable of dealing with that. What I want to know is what are your intentions toward my sister?"

"Intentions?"

Dylan's gloved hands curled into fists at his sides, giving Starbuck the impression that the man, if pushed, could be extremely dangerous. "If you're using her to get to me—"

"I'm not." The idea was so preposterous that Starbuck's shocked honesty was obvious.

"Have you slept with her?"

Before Starbuck could answer honestly in the affirmative, the calm voice of the ecumenical translator explained the idiom.

Grateful for the assistance, he said, "No." It was the truth, so far as it went.

"But you want to."

When Starbuck didn't immediately answer, Dylan said, "I'm a man, damn it, and I know what's in a man's mind when he looks at my sister the way you were looking at Charity."

"Your sister is a very attractive woman."

"She's also a very vulnerable one. I don't want her hurt."

"I have no intention of hurting Charity." This time he was speaking the absolute truth.

"But you do intend to sleep with her."

Reminding himself that he would undoubtedly be acting the same way if some stranger had inappropriately lustful designs on Julianna, Starbuck understood Dylan Prescott's need to protect his sister. But that didn't mean that the man had to be privy to every intimate detail of Charity Prescott's life.

"I don't wish to be rude," he said mildly, "but I do not see where that's really any of your business."

Emotions—irritation, worry, frustration, regret—all ran quickly over Dylan's face and were just as quickly controlled.

"I suppose it's not," he said. "Particularly since she's already been married once, but—"

"Charity was married?"

"Yes. I take it she hasn't filled you in on that horror story yet."

"No, she hasn't." Even as he vowed to learn about Charity's mate at the first opportunity, Starbuck wondered why it suddenly seemed imperative that he know why she was no longer with her legal mate. "I don't suppose you would be willing to enlighten me further."

"No. I wouldn't." Above them, high in the treetops, a jay scolded and went ignored. "But I will tell you this," Dylan advised. "If I ever get my hands on the son of a bitch that used to be her husband, he'll be walking funny for a very long time."

The warning was clear. "I will keep that in mind," Starbuck said.

Dylan nodded. "I'd suggest you do that."

Matters temporarily understood to both men's satisfaction, they began walking back toward the house, following the deep tracks their boots had made.

"You really have no idea what you're doing here?" Dylan asked with a casualness that Starbuck suspected was feigned.

"Not really. Charity thought perhaps I worked at the laboratory."

"If you did, I'd know you."

"Yes. That was my thought, too. Especially since I am an astrophysicist."

Dylan stopped. "Strange that you should remember that."

"Amnesia is an unpredictable thing."

"True." Obviously unconvinced, Dylan began walking again. "Who do you work for?"

"I'm presently between official assignments," Starbuck said. "But I've done some work of my own on antimatter."

Starbuck knew that at this point in time, antimatter existed on earth solely as ephemeral particles created by giant accelerators. It was, in actual operation, more theory than fact.

A theory that would ultimately prove true. When antimatter combined with ordinary matter, mutual annihilation occurred with a force far greater than that produced by thermonuclear fusion.

It had been the fuel of choice for interstellar travel for nearly two centuries. A chunk of it was currently stored in his pocket accelerator.

"Antimatter." Although Dylan didn't slow his pace, Starbuck didn't have to read his mind to know that he was more than a little interested.

"There's been a lot of work done to create antihydrogen," Dylan allowed. "But no one's been able to force an antielectron into orbit around the antiproton."

"It's difficult getting the electrons to fall into stable orbits around atomic nuclei," Starbuck agreed. "However, if one were to draw significant energy from the particles before they are combined—"

"The system would work." Dylan continued striding through the snow, but now his steps were less deliberate, his pace definitely slowed as his mind clicked through the possibilities. "But it would still be difficult to store."

Starbuck had already decided that if he was to return to Sarnia in the proper time, he would need help working out whatever glitch had sent him through the time warp. Such help would be beyond the understanding of most terrans.

Most. But not this man.

Starbuck was just human enough to appreciate fate. And fate, he believed, had brought him to Castle Mountain, Maine. At this point in time.

"Not if it were stored in the form of antihydrogen ice."

That did it. Dylan stopped and stared at him. "At what temperature would it remain stable?"

"Two degrees above absolute zero," Starbuck answered what was common knowledge to any second-level Sarnian. "Held in a container made of ordinary matter at the same temperature, the ice would not explode."

The excitement of scientific discovery held Dylan absolutely still. "And its atoms would annihilate at such a gradual rate that it could be safely stored to last for a very long time," Charity's brother said softly, working out the problem with an alacrity of mind that even Starbuck had not fully expected. "It could even be used for interstellar travel."

He stood there, looking out into the distance, quietly thoughtful. "All those sightings," he murmured. "All those crazy, hysterical reports about little green men."

He turned toward Starbuck. "They were true."

As dangerous as it might turn out to be, Starbuck had decided to trust this man. "Not exactly."

"No." A faint smile curved Dylan's lips. "You are far from little. And not the slightest bit green from what I can tell. Of course, if you'd eaten Charity's pot roast, things might be a little different in that regard." He shook his head. "I have so many questions."

"I thought you might."

"But I haven't the faintest idea where to begin." He rubbed a gloved hand over his cheek. "Where are you from?"

"Sarnia. It's not in your galaxy," he elaborated at Dylan's blank look. He went on to explain, as well as he could without a star chart, the location of his home planet.

"Sarnia. Amazing. Where's your ship, or vehicle, or whatever you call it?"

"I don't have one."

Dylan's shoulders sagged, his disappointment obvious. "I should have known," he muttered. "You're just another kook."

Starbuck decided not to take umbrage at the definition the translator supplied. He wasn't certain that, under the same circumstances, he wouldn't have come to the same conclusion.

"Actually, there are those on my planet who would agree wholeheartedly with you," he admitted. "Especially whenever I attempted to explain my theory of quantum jump physics being a superior means of intergalactic travel."

"Quantum physics?" Dylan asked with studied casualness.

"I had this theory, that the component atoms that make up life could be taken apart, transported through space utilizing the theory of quantum electrodynamics, then be put back together when they'd reached their destination."

"That sounds vaguely familiar." Interest and suspicion warred with each other on Dylan's face. "How do I know that you haven't gotten your hands on a copy of my work in progress?"

"But I have," Starbuck agreed cheerfully. "In fact, your textbook on quantum jump time travel is where I got the idea in the first place."

"I haven't written a book on time travel."

"Not yet. But you will. In fact, it's required reading at the Science Institute. Along with your work on solar flares, of course."

"Solar flares? Never mind," Dylan said quickly. "I'm not sure I want to know this."

He rubbed his chin again with his gloved fingers. "Okay. Let's go through this one step at a time. You allege to be from the planet Sarnia. Perhaps you ought to fill me in on the year."

"Years are calculated differently on Sarnia," Starbuck said. "But from what Charity told me, I seem to have gone back in time a bit on my journey here."

"Charity knows about this?"

"No," Starbuck assured him quickly. "She only knows that she found me, near freezing, on the road yesterday." He frowned. "Although I am extremely grateful, I am not certain it was very wise of her to take a stranger into her home."

"Charity's always been too open for her own good," Dylan said. "When she was a kid, she was always rescuing strays. The house was constantly overrun with animals. It used to drive my parents crazy, but I have to admit, she invariably managed to find homes for all those mangy dogs and cats she dragged home."

Starbuck, who wasn't exactly wild about being compared to a stray dog or cat, remained silent.

"Like that damn cat she's got living with her now," Dylan said. "I remember the day she found it when she was patrolling the waterfront. It was filthy and its fur was matted, but she took it home, gave it a bath, got it shots and now you couldn't get the damn animal out of her house with a hand grenade."

"She said something about the cat owning her," Starbuck recalled.

"She's too softhearted. She even went to law school because she had this wide-eyed optimistic goal about helping the underprivileged," he divulged.

"Charity was an attorney?" Starbuck tried to picture Charity Prescott wearing the stark black robes and grim expressions favored by the barristers on Sarnia and couldn't.

"For a short time. Unfortunately, the system moved too slowly for her, so she decided she could help people more by putting the bad guys behind bars where they couldn't hurt anyone.

"Even after all those years as a cop, dealing with all those criminals, she still manages to see good in almost everything," Dylan said. "And everyone." He shook his head with a mixture of admiration and fraternal worry.

"She believes I have amnesia."

"She might buy that sorry excuse," Dylan said. "Although my sister is twenty-eight years old, she still suffers from a romanticized view of life and people. I used to think she'd grow out of her naiveté, but I've come to the conclusion that she'll probably never entirely throw away her rose-colored glasses . . . and for the record, I didn't believe you for a minute."

"I know. That is one more reason why I decided to trust you with the truth," Starbuck allowed. "Because I knew that you would discover it on your own, anyway."

"What are the other reasons?"

"I can't pass up a chance to work with a man whose name is legendary in the scientific community."

"Legendary?"

Starbuck could tell Dylan Prescott liked that idea. "The name Prescott ranks right up there along with Galileo, Copernicus, Newton, Darwin, Einstein and Pournelle."

"Pournelle?"

"He's a few years down the road."

"Oh." Dylan considered that. "Speaking of which, you still haven't told me what kind of time lag we're talking about here."

"Nearly two hundred of your Earth years. Which is the most important reason I decided to tell you the truth. Even in my era, you have no peers when it comes to your knowledge of time travel. I need your help to build a terran-based transporter. And to work out the coordinates through subspace that will allow me to arrive home in my proper time."

Dylan took a long time to consider the request. "You've no idea how badly I want to believe you. And I honestly don't want to insult you, but you have to remember, I'm a scientist.

"I deal with facts and figures and theorems. I need proof. More than your word about all this," he said apologetically.

"I thought you might." Without so much as a blink of his eye, Starbuck disappeared. The only sign of his former presence was the footprints in the snow. Footprints that abruptly, mysteriously, stopped beside Dylan's.

"Starbuck?" Dylan looked around at the silent woods. "Where the hell are you?"

"Right here."

Dylan spun around on his heel and viewed Starbuck leaning against a tree. An instant later, he was beside him.

"Well?"

Dylan threw back his head and laughed, a bold, hearty laugh that caused the birds on the branches overhead to take flight with a flurry of wings.

"Hot damn," he said. "Beam us up, Scotty, we've got to get to work and figure out a way to send this man home!"

"Then you'll help?"

"I'd like to see you try and stop me." Dylan's gaze immediately sobered. "There's one more thing you should probably know about me. Something you won't find in any book."

Engrossed in already planning his return to Sarnia, Starbuck failed to hear the warning edge to Dylan's tone. "What's that?" he asked absently.

"When Charity was sixteen years old, she began dating the son of a local lobsterman."

Strange how all it took was the woman's name to garner his absolute attention, Starbuck mused. "You didn't approve."

"Not because of what he was," Dylan insisted. "For the record, I'm not an intellectual, or any other kind of snob. What I objected to was the kid's reputation."

"Which was?"

"He was the hometown stud, infamous for scoring with a new girl every Friday night."

"And you didn't want your sister to be one more conquest?"

"Exactly. And I made certain that she wasn't."

"By threatening him?"

"It wasn't a threat. I merely told the horny kid that if he laid one grubby paw on my sister, I would personally cut him into little pieces and use him for bait in his own lobster traps."

"That sounds eminently reasonable," Starbuck agreed. "Under the circumstances."

Dylan couldn't conceal his surprise. "This planet you come from, this Sarnia—"

"Is perfectly peaceful," Starbuck assured him. "We haven't experienced armed conflict for centuries. But I, myself, have an unmarried sister. One I care about very deeply. And if it eases your concerns, you should know that I was, until recently, betrothed to one of my own people."

"That's not entirely reassuring," Dylan argued. "Having split up with your fiancée, you're an ideal candidate for a rebound romance."

"The rift is only temporary." Starbuck frowned as he recalled his former bondmate's cold, final-sounding words. "Sela resented the undue attention my work had attracted, but once I return to Sarnia with proof that my theories were valid, I know she will put aside her objections."

"Oh." Mollified, Dylan's lips curved into a faint smile. "Then we understand one another?"

Against all reason, thoughts of Charity flooded Starbuck's mind. Charity of the soft, fragrant skin, enticing breasts and sparkling eyes.

He remembered the way she'd felt in his arms. The way her warm, open smile could send something dark and forbidden and frightfully primitive surging through his veins.

Tightly garnering the reins of mental control once again, Starbuck reminded himself that he had been bonded to Sela since childhood. Their marriage had always been a foregone conclusion, and Starbuck had not a single doubt that once he regained his lofty position in society, she would honor her end of the betrothal promise.

And even if he weren't planning to marry Sela, Charity Prescott was a terran. She was also the sister of a man who had become, in only a few minutes, not only his lifeline but also his friend.

Forcing down uncharacteristically ambivalent feelings toward Dylan Prescott's twin, Starbuck answered, "Absolutely."

6

CHARITY SENSED the difference in the two men the minute they returned to the kitchen. Her brother was as excited as she'd ever seen him. Starbuck was excited, too, she determined, but he was better at concealing it.

She greeted them with a smile and two cups of steaming coffee. "I was about to send out the Saint Bernards."

"Thank you." Starbuck wrapped his fingers around the warmth of the cup, took a sip and knew what the heaven his mother had always believed in must taste like.

"We were talking," Dylan divulged. "Starbuck remembered he's an astrophysicist."

"Really?" Charity and Vanessa answered in unison.

Charity's eyes narrowed thoughtfully while Vanessa smiled at Starbuck.

"That's quite a coincidence," Vanessa murmured.

"It also might explain what you're doing here," Charity said. "Perhaps you were looking for Dylan, after all."

"He was. But Starbuck's not a recruiter," Dylan said quickly, not giving Starbuck a chance to answer. "It turns out that he's the new man I hired to join the team."

"Oh?" Charity's gaze moved from her brother to Starbuck to Dylan again. "I don't recall anything about a new man."

Dylan shrugged. "I probably forgot to mention it. You know how absentminded I get when I'm engrossed in a project."

That much, at least, was true. But there was something else, Charity thought. Something neither man was prepared to tell her. Deciding that it probably was some sort of hush-hush, ultrasecretive matter, she put it out of her mind.

"Well, it's nice to have that cleared up," she said. "Now all we have to do is find out what happened to all your things and what you were doing out in the middle of the snowstorm."

"He undoubtedly got mugged," Vanessa said helpfully.

"That's probably it," Dylan agreed.

"I agree that it's the most likely answer. But it's also a rather disturbing thought," Charity pointed out. "Since we never have muggings in Castle Mountain."

"There's always a first time," Dylan said cheerfully. Too cheerfully, Charity considered.

"It's still strange."

The toaster popped up. Putting the problem aside for now, Charity took a bagel from the slots, spread it thickly with cream cheese and handed it to Starbuck, who glanced suspiciously at the dark brown ring before taking a tentative bite.

The bagel was hot and chewy, the cheese smooth and cool. The textures and tastes exploded on his tongue. "It's delicious," he declared after he'd finished chewing. "Even better than the coffee."

"Unfortunately, it's also horribly fattening," Vanessa said. She nibbled daintily at her own ungarnished bagel. "You know what they say," she said silkily, "a moment on the lips, a lifetime on the hips."

Her languid, yet pointed gaze slid to Charity, whose bagel, like Starbuck's was spread thickly with cream cheese. "You've no idea how I envy you, Charity, dear. Not many women would permit themselves such a calorie-laden indulgence."

"If you think this is an indulgence, stick around," Charity advised tightly. "I was planning to bring home a pepperoni pizza for dinner."

Vanessa shook her head. "You really should take better care of yourself, Charity. Even if you don't worry about your dress size, I shudder to think what all that fat and cholesterol is doing to your heart."

Starbuck watched the fire flare in Charity's blue eyes, and when he felt it begin to flow through him, as well, he turned his attention to Vanessa Reynolds.

She was severely dressed in black from her head to her feet. Her hair was black, as well, and hung over her shoulders in a shiny curtain. Her dark eyes were lined with a black pencil, a decided contrast to her complexion, which was as pale as the snow on the pine trees outside the window.

Vanessa could have been a genetically designed Sarnian, he mused, as his gaze took in her ascetically slender frame clad in the black tunic and trousers. Her breasts were almost nonexistent and her hips were as slender as a twelve-year-old boy's. She could have been Sela's twin.

As Charity watched Starbuck's slow, thoughtful appraisal of Vanessa Reynolds, a burst of purely feminine pique surged through her like a jolt of lightning.

"Well, speaking of dress sizes, I'd love to sit and chat all day, but I've got to change my clothes and get to work," she said, pushing away from the table.

"And we'd better be getting back to the lab," Dylan said. "Could you drop Starbuck by the lab on your way into town?"

"Are you certain that's wise?" Charity asked with a slight frown. She turned toward Starbuck. "After all you've been through, you should at least spend today in bed."

Starbuck found the suggestion vastly appealing. So long as Charity joined him in that warm wide bed.

Unfortunately, that was not possible.

"I'm feeling fine, Charity," Starbuck assured her.

"Still—"

"I'm a doctor, Charity," Dylan reminded her. "I promise to keep my eye on him all day, in case he starts feeling shaky."

"You won't notice. Not if you're in the throes of scientific creation." Seeds of worry lingered in her eyes.

"Don't worry," Starbuck said, his gaze meeting hers. "I promise to take it easy. But it's important that I join your brother at the lab. And I would be very appreciative if you would drive me there this morning."

"Scientists," she huffed with very real frustration, "you're all crazy." She shook her head, turned away and marched into the bedroom, slamming the door behind her.

"Well, I take it that was a yes," Vanessa drawled.

The obvious derision in her tone irritated Starbuck. "Her concern for others is commendable."

"Concern?" Vanessa laughed at that. "Oh, I think it's a great deal more than concern that has Charity forgetting her manners." She smiled up at Starbuck as she rose and began pulling on her gloves. "I'll see you later." Wagging her fingers, she left the kitchen.

Dylan stood in the open doorway, letting cold air into the house as his gaze went from Starbuck to the closed bedroom door to Starbuck again.

"Your brotherly concern is unnecessary," Starbuck said quietly. "I have already promised not to hurt her."

"I believe you mean that." Dylan's expression was grim. "But if you were to stick around Earth for a while, Starbuck, you'd realize that humans—especially the female of the species—are by nature, subjective, emotional and highly unpredictable. Which makes it difficult, if not impossible, to deal with them in an objective, quantitative fashion."

"My mother is a terran," Starbuck felt obliged to point out. "A human," he explained at Dylan's puzzled look.

"Really?" Observing the glint in Dylan's eyes, Starbuck had the feeling that scientific curiosity had just temporarily overridden Dylan's concern for his sister's emotional well-being.

"Truly," Starbuck assured him. "Although intermarriage is rare between the ruling classes on Sarnia, my father broke tradition by bringing back a bride from one of his diplomatic missions to Earth. Both Julianna, my sister, and I are half terran and half Sarnian."

"I can't wait to get you on an examining table," Dylan enthused. Outside, Vanessa called to him, complaining about waiting in the cold. "I'm coming," Dylan called out to her.

Then, just when Starbuck thought the conversation was over, Dylan warned, "Don't hurt her." And then he was gone, wading his way through the snow to the black machine.

THIS WAS RIDICULOUS, Charity told herself. She didn't even know Starbuck. Not really. He was merely a man she'd rescued in the line of duty. There was nothing personal in their relationship, for heaven's sake.

Well, there had been that little incident this morning, she allowed as she changed from her angora sweater and jeans into her winter-weight blue uniform. But that had merely been an anomaly, two people sharing a bed caught up in their own sensual dreams. It could have happened with anyone.

But it hadn't. It had happened with Bram Starbuck, and although she'd sworn never to get involved with another good-looking man again, Charity recognized her own vulnerability.

As if born of her own unhappy, tumultuous thoughts, there was a knock on the door. "Charity?" the deep voice called. "Is everything all right?"

"Everything's just hunky-dory," she called back to him.

There was a moment's silence. "May I come in?"

She was pinning on the five-sided star that her father had proudly worn for thirty-two years. "I'll be right out."

Vulnerable she might be, but she wasn't a total idiot. Not so much that she'd be alone in this room with a man who could, with a single glance, create such havoc with her senses.

Ignoring her pointed hint, Starbuck opened the door and stood there in the doorway, observing her with his probing dark gaze.

"Vanessa upset you," he diagnosed.

"Don't be silly," she said in a trembling undertone that told Starbuck she was lying. "I told you, Starbuck, I just get bad vibes from the woman."

"So do I." Without waiting for an invitation, he crossed the room and stood in front of her.

"Do you?"

"Yes." Charity heard the absolute honesty in the single word, saw it in his eyes. "But I have a feeling that this is about more than bad vibrations," Starbuck suggested.

"No, really—"

When she would have turned away, he caught her chin in his hand. Closely, calmly, he examined her. "What's wrong?" The warmth of his touch sent a new flood of emotions bubbling through her.

"It's just that she's so damn thin."

"Yes. She is."

He didn't have to agree so fast, she thought miserably. "And I'm not."

"That is also true." His gaze, as it moved from her face to take a slow, judicious tour of her body, set her nerves to ringing like bells inside her head. "I still do not understand."

She ran an agitated hand through her hair, frustrated at him, at herself, at this unsettling situation she seemed to have found herself in. "Men like thin women."

"Ah." Starbuck understood that for some ridiculously emotional, undoubtedly female reason, she felt physically inadequate when compared to Vanessa Reynolds. "Would it make you feel any better if I told you that I'm not like other men you have known?" Now that, he decided with grim humor, had to be the understatement of the millennium.

"Not really." Reminding herself that she was on the verge of making a very big mistake, Charity freed herself from his light hold and began backing away.

"What if I told you that I find your body very appealing?" Starbuck took a step toward her. "Just as it is."

Charity took another backward step. "If that's supposed to make me feel more comfortable around you, it doesn't."

"I was afraid of that." When she continued to back away, Starbuck matched his steps to hers. "Your brother told me that you'd been married."

The backs of her knees were pressing against the bed where she'd awakened in his arms. Short of scrambling over the top of the mattress, she was effectively trapped.

"So?"

"He also informed me that your husband hurt you."

"Dylan had no right to tell you that," Charity flared.

"I think he did." Starbuck sighed. "He wanted to make certain that this didn't happen."

"That what didn't happen?" Charity was experiencing a nervous, edgy kind of excitement like nothing she'd ever known.

He lifted a hand to her cheek. His eyes were dark and strangely sad. "Me wanting you. You wanting me."

"Well." Charity let out a breath she'd been unaware of holding. "You certainly don't beat around the bush, do you?"

Starbuck grasped the meaning an instant before the translator decoded it for him. His knowledge of English idioms, he considered with a burst of un-Sarnian pride, was improving.

"No. I don't."

In contrast to Vanessa's ice, Charity was heat. From the bright sunset color of her hair, to her golden complexion, to her full rose-hued lips, to the intriguing color that rose periodically in her cheeks, as it was now.

Her scent was surrounding him like a particularly fragrant ether cloud; her skin was soft against the palm of his hand. Starbuck's mind was in a disorderly turmoil. He was embarrassed to find himself so uncharacteristically distracted, but that only made the turmoil worse.

"What makes you think I want you?" Charity's voice was steady, her heart was not.

"Don't you?"

He ran a fingertip over her lips before either of them realized his intentions. When they parted instinctively at his touch, Starbuck reminded himself that even an emotion-driven terran male would be cautious enough to take a pace back to consider his actions before he stepped off the edge of a cliff.

"I'm sorry," Starbuck said gruffly. To give himself some much needed distance, he backed away and began to roam the room. "I had no right to ask that question. Just as I had no right to touch you in such a familiar manner."

He opened an opaque white jar and scooped a bit of the pink cream onto his finger. It carried her scent; Starbuck was struck with a sudden, almost uncontrollable urge to rub that cream into her smooth, round breasts.

Telling herself it was only because Starbuck was so unflinchingly honest, Charity decided to tell the truth now.

"Then why does it feel as if you do?"

Desire hit like the fiery jolt of a laser blast in the gut. Starbuck controlled it ruthlessly, pushing it down and away from his conscious mind.

"Dylan will be waiting."

Charity waited until her voice would be properly calm. And professional. "And I need to get to work."

"To your police station."

So they were back to that again. "Yes." Her chin tilted up in a challenge, daring him to make one chauvinistic remark. "To my police station."

Although she'd always prided herself on being a remarkably easygoing person, Charity found that irritation, even anger, was turning out to be a great deal more comfortable than these other emotions he was stimulating.

Starbuck's eyes swept over her again, clad in the sexless blue wool shirt and trousers. "I much prefer that tunic you were wearing this morning."

"Tunic? Oh, my sweater." It figured Bram Starbuck would prefer his women in something pink and fluffy.

The thought had no sooner crossed her mind than Charity brought herself up sharply. She was not *his* woman.

"Well, I really hate to disappoint you, Starbuck, but pink isn't really much of an authority color."

"I can appreciate that." He nodded. "But if you think that uniform will make a man forget that you're a woman—a very, sensual, desirable woman—Charity Prescott, you're mistaken."

Against all reason, against every atom of his common sense, Starbuck came to stand in front of her again. His hand cupped her neck, slid into the silk of her hair.

"On the contrary," he murmured, "it makes a man want to strip it off, piece by stiff, ugly piece, and discover whatever soft feminine secrets you are trying so hard to conceal."

It took a major effort of will, but Charity managed to restrain herself from either melting into his arms or from pulling away. In the instant she had to make her decision, she decided that to run for cover would make her look vulnerable.

So she simply stood there, looking up at him. Watching. Waiting.

Starbuck lowered his lips to within a whisper of hers, then hesitated. His logical mind, the part of him that knew this could be a fatal mistake, wanted to allow her to back away now. Before they found themselves in a relationship neither one of them wanted nor could afford.

The emotional, often distressing human side to his nature, the part of him that had irrationally become linked to her from the moment he'd entered her fantasy and had been pulled into a place so different from his intended destination, knew she would not move away.

The moment his lips brushed against hers, Starbuck realized exactly how badly he'd miscalculated. He'd intended to control the kiss like an experiment. After observing her carefully, he'd thought Charity would be cool and calm and sweet.

Sweet she most definitely was. But cool? Calm? There was nothing cool about the mouth that clung so hungrily to his. There was nothing calm about the hands that thrust into his hair. All his earlier hypotheses flew out the window as he felt the heat flare, the passion rise.

There was something mindless happening here. Something dark and dangerous. Something he couldn't analyze. Sense was seeping out of him. Logic disintegrated. Starbuck found himself lost in a smoky, turbulent world like nothing he'd ever known.

It could have been a minute, an hour, an eternity. When he finally took his mouth from hers, Starbuck realized that his hands, which had taken hold of her shoulders sometime during that heated kiss, were far from steady.

He wanted her now. Immediately. Desperately. He wanted to drag her to the bed, or the nearest chair, or even the hard oak plank floor, and strip that thick dark uniform she wore like armor away and bury himself deep inside her welcoming warmth.

When he realized that sometime during that shared kiss desire had come dangerously close to metamorphosing into need, he backed away.

"Well," she said after a few seconds. "That was . . . uh . . . certainly different."

So she'd felt it, too. He'd wondered but had been too rattled at the time to read her emotions. "Yes. It was."

They stared at each other.

Charity swallowed. "It could also be a problem."

"Only if we let it."

For not the first time since she'd dragged him into her Jeep, her home, her bed, not to mention her life, Charity wondered what kind of man Starbuck was.

What type of man could kiss her with a passion that threatened to set the world on fire, then immediately turn so cool and controlled? A calculating one, she decided.

He watched her face close up, folding like the petals of a moonflower as the shadows of night approached. As she went over to the dresser and scooped a handful of coins into her trouser pockets, Starbuck saw that her hands shook.

She was right, Starbuck admitted reluctantly. This could be one herculean problem.

"I want to make love to you, Charity," he told her with a stiff politeness that took every ounce of his self-control. With truth came reason, Starbuck reminded himself. With reason came truth. Once Charity understood his motivation, she would undoubtedly cease to be so upset. "Very much. But I promised your brother that I would not."

"What?" She spun around and shot him an unbelieving look. "What does Dylan have to do with this?"

The anger was radiating off her in waves. Deciding that this was one more instance where he'd gravely miscalculated, Starbuck took a deep breath and tried again.

"I explained that he told me about your husband."

"Steven is my ex-husband," Charity corrected sharply.

"I also explained that Dylan informed me that your husband, ex-husband," he amended at her blistering look, "did something that hurt you. And since your brother cares for you very much, he made me promise that I would not permit you to become emotionally involved with me."

"Not permit me?" Her voice rose higher, like a soprano practicing her scales. "Are you saying that Dylan made you promise not to permit me to become emotionally involved with you?"

"Yes. That is precisely what I'm saying."

She folded her arms across the front of the uniform shirt. "And I suppose you agreed."

"Of course."

Once again Starbuck found the human feminine mind to be a mystery. He'd explained their situation. So why did she appear to be so furious? She reminded him of one of the smoking, simmering volcanoes on the planet Pele, just prior to eruption.

Charity nodded. "Of course," she murmured scathingly. "Lucky for you he wasn't prepared to marry me off. Lord knows how many camels he'd ask for."

"Camels?"

After explaining that she was referring to a two-humped ruminant quadruped of the genus *Camelus*, the translator, obviously as stumped as Starbuck was by Charity's reference, turned frustratingly silent.

"We did not discuss any camels," he protested.

"You've no idea what a relief that is," she shot back. Cursing under her breath, she marched from the room.

Starbuck followed, coming to an abrupt halt when he saw what she was buckling around her waist.

She followed his startled gaze to the leather holster at her hip. "Haven't you ever seen a Smith & Wesson .38 before?"

"Not at such close range."

The few antique weapons he had been privileged to see had always been locked away in glass cases in government archives that required the highest security clearances.

"And not worn by a woman, either," she suggested acidly.

"No."

"I can imagine that would prove discomfiting."

"Actually, it does."

In theory, and put in the larger context of history, Starbuck had always found the primitive weapons used by other, more violent societies undeniably fascinating.

Now, forced to accept the danger such a revolver represented to a woman he already cared for a great deal more than he should, Starbuck found it unreasonably terrifying.

"Now, why doesn't that surprise me?" She pulled her jacket down from a peg by the door, shrugged into it and said, "If you're coming, let's go."

Scooping up the jacket Dylan had loaned him, Starbuck obediently followed.

They drove down the snowy road in silence. Having grown up beneath a climatically controlled domed city, where plants and animals were cultivated solely for consumption by the lower-class workers, Starbuck found the Maine tree-studded countryside a revelation.

Within five minutes he had caught sight of innumerable birds, a white snowshoe hare similar to the ones on the planet Polaris, several bushy-tailed squirrels, and a furry flat-tailed animal his memory banks told him was a beaver.

He would have been having a wonderful time were it not for Charity's uncharacteristically stony silence. As the dashboard odometer clicked away the distance in tenths of miles, Starbuck grew more and more uncomfortable.

"I'm sorry I kissed you."

"Don't you dare apologize." Charity didn't take her eyes from the road, slowing slightly when a red fox suddenly sprinted out of the trees and ran in front of the Jeep, its mahogany coat contrasting brightly with the sparkling white snow.

"All right."

As the fox disappeared behind the curtain of pine trees on the other side of the road, Starbuck decided that he was going to ask Dylan for the secret to what went on inside an Earth woman's seemingly unfathomable mind. After all, he was about to reveal the practical application of antimatter to the man; such exchange of information would only be fair.

"Would it make you angry if I told you that I was sorry for apologizing?"

Charity's lips curved into a reluctant smile. "The reason you don't have to apologize is because I enjoyed it."

"Oh. I thought, at the time, that you did," Starbuck allowed. "But if you enjoyed kissing me, why are you so angry?"

Because I enjoyed it too much, she could have answered, but didn't. "Because of the chauvinistic way you and Dylan talked about me as if I were some precious piece of porcelain that had to be handled properly for fear of breaking."

Starbuck considered that. "He was only trying to protect you, Charity. I would do the same for my sister."

She slanted him a sideways glance. "You have a sister?"

"Yes."

"What does she do? For a living?"

"She's a xenoanthropologist."

"A what?"

Belatedly realizing that this society did not yet have a need for people who studied alien cultures found on other planets and galaxies, he said, "It's a kind of anthropologist."

"Oh." Charity nodded. "Sounds as if she's pretty smart."

"Oh, yes. She's quite extraordinary."

"For a woman?" she asked.

"I didn't say that," he reminded her mildly. "Actually, Julianna is one of the most intelligent persons—male or female—that I've ever known."

"Maybe there's hope for you yet," Charity decided. "Is she younger or older than you?"

"Younger. But only by a few years."

"So, although she's one of the most intelligent persons—male or female—" she threw his words back at him, "you've ever known, you still feel the need to protect her."

"Of course."

"Because she's a woman."

"That's right." He was becoming uncomfortable. The conversation was more than a little familiar. It was one he'd had with Julianna on too many occasions.

"What if she were your younger brother?" Charity asked.

"I don't have a younger brother," Starbuck pointed out with perfect logic. "I told you, Charity, Julianna is my sister."

Charity's frustrated sigh ruffled her coppery bangs. "Let's try a hypothetical," she suggested. "As a scientist, I'm sure you understand how hypothesis works."

He thought he detected sarcasm in her tone, but decided not to mention it while she was so obviously irritated. "Of course."

"Fine." Charity nodded. "So, let's say—hypothetically speaking—that Julianna is now Julien, your younger brother."

"All right. Hypothetically speaking."

"And Julien met a woman who he found attractive. A woman who found him equally appealing. Are you with me so far?"

"Absolutely."

"Would you feel the need to go to this woman and warn her to stay away from Julien? In order to protect him?"

"Of course not."

"Because he's a man."

"Yes."

Charity was undeniably charming. And, knowing she'd been an attorney, Starbuck allowed that she was also intelligent. So why couldn't she see the simple logic of his reasoning?

"I give up." Obviously frustrated, Charity threw both hands in the air, causing the Jeep, which had just hit a patch of ice, to veer dangerously toward the edge of the road.

"Damn." Grabbing hold of the steering wheel, she deftly maneuvered the truck back into the middle of the packed snow with a skill that Starbuck couldn't help but admire.

"That was very good," he said, hoping to deflate her anger.

"I've had very good training."

She turned a corner and suddenly a building that had been hidden away in a grove of pine trees came into view. It crossed Starbuck's mind that if he hadn't known the laboratory was here, he never would have found it.

"Well, here we are. Safe and sound."

Sound, perhaps, Starbuck agreed silently. But far from safe. Because they were rapidly approaching something that could prove inordinately dangerous.

"Thank you. I appreciate your driving me here."

She shrugged. "There wasn't room for three on the snowmobile. And although you make me want to throw things at your chauvinistic head, Starbuck, I'd rather put up with your frustrating, maddening company than Vanessa's smug superiority."

"Is that a backhanded compliment?"

"I suppose it is." The smile he was rapidly becoming addicted to bloomed on her lips, in her eyes.

"In that case . . ."

Leaning toward her, he touched her face. Not seductively, not soothingly, but with a masculine possessiveness that he half expected to anger her all over again, but, for some reason he couldn't comprehend, didn't.

"I like your company, too, Charity." When he brushed the pad of his thumb against her lip, Starbuck felt a jolt of reaction and was unsure whether it was hers or his.

"Very much, as a matter of fact." He watched her lips part on a trembling sigh. "And you know what else?"

Her eyes had drifted closed in anticipation of his kiss. Her lashes were a thick fringe against her cheek. "What?"

"You are probably correct, when you refer to me as a chauvinist, but I am also very glad that you're a woman."

She tasted exactly the way a woman should taste. And her lips felt exactly the way a woman's lips should feel—soft and warm and generous. Starbuck decided that he could drink from them forever.

When her right hand leaned across the space between them and gripped the front of his coat, he decided that once again they were sharing the same thought.

He ran kisses over her upturned face as emotion stronger than anything he'd ever felt before swelled in him.

Starbuck's first thought was that he was falling in love. But that was impossible. Every Sarnian knew that the term was an outdated euphemism for something a great deal more biological. But even knowing that couldn't quite diminish the strange feeling that he'd come all the way through time and space specifically to meet this woman.

Outside the Jeep, the snow had begun to fall again, soft white flakes that drifted to earth like floating petals. Inside, there were low murmurs and soft sighs.

"Your brother's going to wonder where I am," he murmured as his lips brushed over her ear.

"Dylan's an intelligent man," she said on a soft sigh as his lips pressed warmly against her temple. "He'll figure it out."

"That's what I'm afraid of."

Although it was the hardest thing he'd ever done, Starbuck backed away, figuratively and emotionally from what was quickly becoming a highly illogical, extremely volatile situation.

Her lips, slightly swollen and darkly pink, curved upward in a reassuring smile. Her anger, Starbuck noted, was like a shooting star: a quick, hot flare and then it was gone.

"I'm twenty-eight years old, Starbuck," she told him. "And as much as Dylan might dearly like to think otherwise, what I do or whom I do it with, is none of my brother's business."

Leaning forward, she brushed her lips against his. "Have a good day in the brain factory. I'll try to run down your stuff. See you later."

"Later," Starbuck agreed. If he found being alone with Charity distracting, he was appalled at his reluctance to leave her. "Despite what I promised your brother, I still want you."

"I know."

"I've also discovered, against all logical reason, that I need you. And such need terrifies me."

Her gaze softened and she touched a hand to his cheek to soothe. "I know that, too."

"I rather thought you did," Starbuck agreed. "Since we inexplicably seem to share the same thoughts quite often." His eyes remained on hers as he resisted the urge to draw her close for another taste. "You were correct about it being a problem."

"Yes." She could not deny that.

"But we'll deal with it."

She nodded, her heart in her eyes. "Yes."

It was only after he'd kissed her goodbye one last time and was walking toward the door of the laboratory that Starbuck realized what it was that Charity had just agreed to.

Making love to Charity, after he'd specifically promised her brother not to, would not only be unethical and illogical, it would be insane.

Dylan Prescott held the key to Starbuck's very survival. Without him to correct the time sequence, Starbuck could very well arrive home during the wrong time. Even before the Ancient Ones had arrived with their superior intellect and laws and reason, and civilized what had once been an inhospitable, primitive planet.

And that would be suicide.

So what was it about Charity that had Starbuck willing to risk exactly that?

NO RISK, NO OBLIGATION TO BUY...NOW OR EVER!

CASINO JUBILEE
"Scratch'n Match" Game

Here's how to play:

1. Peel off label from front cover. Place it in space provided at right. With a coin, carefully scratch off the silver box. This makes you eligible to receive two or more free books, and possibly another gift, depending upon what is revealed beneath the scratch-off area.

2. You'll receive brand-new Harlequin Temptation® novels. When you return this card, we'll rush you the books and gift you qualify for, **ABSOLUTELY FREE!**

3. Then, if we don't hear from you, every month we'll send you 4 additional novels to read and enjoy, before they are available in bookstores. You can return them and owe nothing, but if you decide to keep them, you'll pay only $2.44* each plus 25¢ delivery and applicable sales tax, if any*. That's the complete price, and— compared to cover prices of $2.99 each in stores—quite a bargain!

4. When you join the Harlequin Reader Service®, you'll get our subscribers-only newsletter, as well as additional free gifts from time to time, just for being a subscriber!

5. You must be completely satisfied. You may cancel at any time simply by sending us a note or a shipping statement marked ''cancel'' or by returning any shipment to us at our cost.

YOURS FREE!

This lovely heart-shaped box is richly detailed with cut-glass decorations, perfect for holding a precious memento or keepsake—and it's yours absolutely free when you accept our no-risk offer.

CASINO JUBILEE
"Scratch'n Match" Game

SCRATCH HERE

CHECK CLAIM CHART BELOW
FOR YOUR FREE GIFTS!

YES! I have placed my label from the front cover in the space provided above and scratched off the silver box. Please send me all the gifts for which I qualify. I understand I am under no obligation to purchase any books, as explained on the opposite page.

142 CIH AH2X (U-H-T-02/93)

Name _____

Address _____ Apt. _____

City _____ State _____ Zip _____

▼ DETACH AND MAIL CARD TODAY! ▼

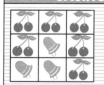

◀ DETACH AND MAIL CARD TODAY! ◀

BUSINESS REPLY MAIL
FIRST CLASS MAIL   PERMIT NO. 717   BUFFALO, NY

POSTAGE WILL BE PAID BY ADDRESSEE

HARLEQUIN READER SERVICE
3010 WALDEN AVE
PO BOX 1867
BUFFALO NY 14240-9952

NO POSTAGE
NECESSARY
IF MAILED
IN THE
UNITED STATES

Like all scientists, Starbuck had always enjoyed solving problems. Even as a boy, he'd enjoyed puzzles, the more complicated the better. He enjoyed dissecting a problem, pulling it apart piece by piece until finally, after meticulous study, he would have the answer.

He knew, that with diligence and Dylan's help, he would solve the puzzle of time and distance and return safely to his planet.

Unfortunately, the answer to his more personal dilemma, Starbuck suspected, could not be solved by logic or scientific method. In horror, he realized he was reacting more like a human than a proper Sarnian. But he couldn't remember when he'd enjoyed anything more than he'd enjoyed kissing Charity.

A problem she might be, he acknowledged honestly. But she was the most delectable, enticing, delightful problem he'd ever encountered.

7

THE LABORATORY, unsurprisingly, was tightly secured. Starbuck stood in front of the all-seeing eye of the video camera and was about to press the button to the intercom when the front door suddenly slid open.

"Well, hello," Vanessa greeted him. "I was wondering when you'd show up." She glanced over Starbuck's shoulder. "I suppose Charity's on her way to work."

"Yes." Once again Starbuck found himself uncomfortable with the polite small talk that seemed to be the custom on this planet. "To her police station."

"For the life of me, I can't imagine why any woman would want to be a police officer," Vanessa said.

"Nor can I," Starbuck responded.

Vanessa rewarded him with a slow, distinctly feminine smile that made Starbuck think that perhaps Dylan hadn't claimed this woman, after all.

"I mean, it's such an unfeminine occupation," she said. "Don't you think?"

He did. But there was a predatory glint in her dark eyes that had him feeling decidedly uncomfortable. That and the way this woman made Charity feel inferior had Starbuck avoiding a direct answer.

"I think Charity is the most feminine woman I've ever met." He'd never, in all his thirty years, uttered a more truthful statement.

"Well." Her smile turned cold; frost tinged her eyes. "You can't blame a girl for trying, now, can you?"

"No. You can't."

She gave him a curious look tinged with renewed humor. "You're a strange one, Starbuck. But then again, aren't we all?"

She pulled on a pair of thick leather gloves. "I'm going for a walk," she divulged. "A brisk stroll through the woods always clears my head when I'm stumped. Go on in," she said. "The receptionist at the front desk will page Dylan for you and take care of getting you a proper ID."

That said, she left the building, walking away without a backward glance. Starbuck watched for a moment, wondering why it was that the smooth movement of her hips did not affect him in the way Charity's did.

Then, deciding to dwell on that question later, he entered the building.

Starbuck was not surprised when Dylan's laboratory turned out to be far more advanced than his time. The textbooks had claimed that Dylan Prescott was extraordinary, and after spending a morning listening to him explain how he'd come up with his idea of quantum physics providing the key to time travel, Starbuck was more than a little inclined to agree.

It didn't take long for them to come to the conclusions that the magnetic electrical field caused by the solar flares had undoubtedly been the cause of him going off track as he'd slid around the folds and warps of subspace that had allowed him to cut across the light-years.

While Starbuck felt perfectly comfortable with that logical hypothesis, there was something else troubling him. Something he was not prepared to share with Dylan.

Because the errant thought teasing at the far reaches
of his mind was that perhaps solar flares were not the
only answer. What if—and this was admittedly far-
fetched—he'd been drawn here by Charity? By her
fantasy?

The idea was too unsettling and illogical to be taken
seriously. But still, as hard as he tried, Starbuck found
it impossible to completely dismiss.

THREE DAYS AFTER rescuing Starbuck from the blizzard, Charity was more stumped than ever. None of his
belongings had shown up anywhere on the island. No
one could remember seeing him before she'd discovered him on the road. And since strangers were a rarity
in this remote little corner of the world, especially in the
winter, she was forced to conclude that he'd been
mugged on the mainland, taken to Castle Mountain
and dumped.

But by whom? And why?

None of the New England police departments had
any report of a man fitting Starbuck's description reported missing. Nor were there any outstanding war-
rants for a man named Bram Starbuck. It was almost
as if he'd dropped into her life from the blue.

Starbuck. Charity sipped her coffee and drummed
her fingers on the scarred wooden arms of her father's
old chair as she tried to sort her professional feelings for
the dark, mysterious stranger from her personal ones.

The policewoman in Charity was irritated that she
hadn't solved a simple missing-persons case. The
woman in her couldn't stop thinking of the way his eyes
darkened with sensual intent whenever he looked at
her. The police chief had decided to extend her queries
to New York; the woman wondered what it would be

like to lie with the man in front of a roaring fire while a blizzard raged outside.

Not that she'd ever know. Because the man seemed determined to honor that damn promise to Dylan. For the past three days Starbuck had spent almost every waking hour at the laboratory. At night, he slept in the loft, arriving home long after she had finally given up waiting for him and fallen asleep.

Each morning, he would be dressed with the coffee made by the time she got up. And on those rare occasions they found themselves alone together, he conveniently thought of something, somewhere else, that urgently needed doing.

That he was avoiding her was more than a little obvious.

What was so distressing was exactly how badly that hurt.

She was vowing, for the umpteenth time, to simply treat him like any other police case, when the phone rang.

"Police department."

Just what she needed, Charity thought with an inner groan as the voice reported a fight at a local tavern. A waterfront brawl.

Her deputy, Andy Mayfair, had gone to lunch, claiming a sudden hankering for Nicolette Dupree's Wednesday afternoon chowder at the Gray Gull café. From the way the fifty-five-year-old man blushed whenever Nicolette's name was mentioned, Charity had the feeling that he was interested in a lot more than clam chowder.

Hating to disturb him, Charity dialed the number of his beeper. When she didn't get an answer, she realized he'd left it on the front seat of the truck. Again.

That left her two choices. Since the Gray Gull was in the opposite direction of the harbor, she could waste much needed time to drive by the café to pick up her deputy. Or she could handle things herself. The day she couldn't handle a few drunks was the day she'd hang up her father's badge.

Making her decision, Charity left the warmth of the police station, climbed into the Jeep and headed toward the waterfront.

STARBUCK AND DYLAN HAD just finished running a program when Dylan said, "We've worked past lunch. You must be starving."

Starbuck was surprised at how much time had flown. "I am hungry."

Dylan stood up and stretched. "There's some left-over pizza in the fridge. We can heat it up in the microwave. Unless you'd like something else."

"Pizza is fine," Starbuck said, not having any idea what he had just agreed to, but since so far, everything on Earth—most especially some magical mixture called peanut butter—tasted wonderful, he was eager to try something new.

This was even better than wonderful, Starbuck decided ten minutes later. Although the too-hot cheese had burned the roof of his mouth, he found the combination of textures and taste to be a gastronomical delight.

He was considering the logistics of taking a lifetime supply of frozen pizzas back to Sarnia with him when Vanessa appeared in the doorway of the lunchroom.

"Would you two gentlemen mind if I joined you?"

"Of course not," Dylan said.

"I didn't want to interrupt your work," she said. Her husky voice reminded Starbuck of the purr of a polar-cat. And as she entered the room on that loose-limbed glide, he decided the feline analogy definitely fit.

"All you're interrupting is a discussion of the wonders of pepperoni," Dylan informed her.

She glanced down at the cheese-stained cardboard box with obvious disdain. "You and your sister have the most horrendous eating habits."

Dylan grinned. "I'd rather live to be eighty eating pizza than one hundred eating the Styrofoam disks you live on."

"Rice cakes are very nutritious." As Starbuck watched, she took a package down from a shelf. "Would you care for one?"

"That would be very nice," Starbuck answered politely. How bad could it be?

A moment later, he found out exactly how bad. "It's very good," he said, chasing the dry hard chips with a swallow of the effervescent cola Dylan had introduced him to.

"And you're a liar," Vanessa responded, her tone as dry as the rice cake Starbuck was having difficulty swallowing. "But a handsome one." She smiled over at Dylan. "How are things going?"

"About as good as can be expected," Dylan answered obliquely. "How's Emily coming along?"

"I was hoping for a cell split this morning, but something went wrong. Again. But I took a little walk to clear my head and I think I've got this latest bug worked out."

"Well, good luck," Dylan said.

"Thanks. At this stage in the cloning process, I'm going to need all the luck I can get." Glancing down at her watch, she sighed and said, "But since luck alone won't do it, I'd better get back to work."

She paused in the doorway. "Will you be working late?"

From the obvious invitation in her tone, Starbuck knew that it was not scientific curiosity that had her asking the question. He'd observed over the past three days that Vanessa Reynolds and Dylan Prescott were a great deal more than mere platonic friends.

"Probably." Dylan exchanged a look with Starbuck. "We have a lot to do."

"I felt like cooking tonight. And it's no fun to cook for one." Her voice, Starbuck noticed, had deepened once again to its throaty polarcat purr.

"Sorry, but I think I'd better take a rain check." Dylan offered Vanessa a conciliatory smile.

Small white tension lines appeared around her pale lips. Her eyes hardened. "Of course. Far be it from me to interfere with genius."

The word was flung at him like an epithet. Then she stalked from the room.

Dylan sighed. "Women."

"She seems to care for you," Starbuck observed, even as it crossed his mind that he hadn't seen that same light of desire in Vanessa's eyes that burned so brightly in Charity's whenever she looked at him.

"I thought so, too, in the beginning," Dylan agreed with a shrug. "But lately I've come to the conclusion that she uses sex in the same way she climbs her stair-stepper for an hour every morning. As an exercise designed to burn off dreaded calories.

"But Vanessa can be exciting, in her own way," he added. "And I can't deny that she's smart as a whip."

"She said she was working on genetics?"

"Yeah. She's trying to clone Emily Brontë."

"Emily Brontë?" The name rang a bell.

"Yeah, you know, the novelist. Actually, thinking about it, you probably don't know. The woman wrote *Wuthering Heights* back in the 1800s.

"Apparently Vanessa bought a locket at a flea market in London a few years back that turns out to have been owned by Branwell Brontë, the brother. There was a lock of dark hair in the locket that Vanessa believes is Emily's. So, she's determined to clone herself a new romance novelist."

"Emily Brontë," Starbuck mused. "Of course." He nodded. "I thought, when Vanessa called me Heathcliff, that the name was vaguely familiar. My mother has a copy of that novel."

"An actual copy? Bound and everything?" Dylan, who'd never been interested in money, unless he was trying to scrounge up funds for his work, couldn't help thinking how much that little gem would be worth two centuries from now.

"The book is a family heirloom," Starbuck said. "Although it is rather the worse for wear. My father cringed every time she read it because such frequent use made more pages fall out."

"I can imagine." Dylan shook his head. "Sounds as if your mother's a romantic."

"I suppose that would describe her," Starbuck agreed.

"What about your sister? Is she a romantic, too?"

"Oh, Julianna is definitely nothing like Mother," Starbuck said quickly. "She inherited far more of our father's traits than I did, although she is, unfortunately, mindblind."

"Mindblind?"

"Most Sarnians possess telepathy," Starbuck explained. "Especially those descended from the Ancient Ones, as my father's house is. Unfortunately, Julianna does not."

"Do you?"

"Yes, although I've been finding it increasingly difficult since I arrived here on Earth. For example, I have received what Charity referred to as vibes from Vanessa, yet I cannot determine what, exactly, she's thinking."

"That's probably just as well," Dylan decided. "How about me? Can you read my mind?"

"I don't know. Sarnians are taught at an early age that it is not polite to enter one's thoughts unless invited."

"So now you're invited." Dylan leaned back, crossed his legs at the ankles and waited. "Give it your best shot."

Something was definitely blocking Dylan's brain waves. Starbuck looked at him, baffled. "I can't." He tried again, then ran his hand through his hair, frustrated. "I don't understand."

"Perhaps it's the difference in atmosphere."

"Perhaps," Starbuck agreed, unconvinced. "This inability is decidedly unwelcome. If I were Julianna, I would become very frustrated."

"And she doesn't?"

"Oh, no. Julianna would never get frustrated. She is unfailingly cool and calm, and logical to a fault. Logical for a woman, that is," he felt obliged to add. "She does have distressingly strong feelings concerning feminine equality."

Dylan laughed at that as he gathered up the paper napkins, the pizza box and the two red-and-white cans, putting them into the proper recycling bins.

"Sounds like Charity. It seems we've got a lot more than our work in common, Starbuck."

"More than you think," Starbuck muttered. "Since both our sisters insist in pursuing work that is potentially dangerous."

"Dangerous?"

Starbuck sighed as he thought about his sister's secret quest. "During a recent research excursion, Julianna discovered a packet of documents defaming the Ancient Ones."

"Your ancestors were among the Ancient Ones," Dylan recalled.

"That's true. And our history reveres them for bringing peace and reason to a savage, uncivilized planet." His frown darkened to a scowl. "But Julianna insists that she's found a diary alleging that a vibrant, matriarchal society existed on Sarnia long before the arrival of our ancestors. It also claims the Ancient Ones came, not in peace, but at the bequest of the husband of the Elder Mother—the planet's ruler."

"Yours certainly wouldn't be the first society to fudge when writing its history books."

"True. But if Julianna's documents prove legitimate, our entire system of belief and laws is based on a falsehood. The diary claims women ruled Sarnia in peace and prosperity for several centuries with a vision of equality for all."

"That is a bit different from what you've told me about Sarnia's past," Dylan allowed.

"It gets worse. Julianna also has letters alleging that Elder Mother's husband—with assistance from our ancestors—initiated a bloody purge to gain absolute control.

"And when it was over, to ensure that the females would not be allowed to reestablish their claim, members of the original ruling families were brutally killed. Or, in the case of children, banished to the moon Australiana, which eventually became a penal colony for those individuals who could not adapt to the strict rules of Sarnian law. A law based on logic and reason. And the unequivocable biological superiority of males."

Dylan whistled softly. "If those papers really are legitimate, your sister is sitting on a virtual powder keg."

Starbuck cursed and dragged his hand through his hair. "If anyone at the institute discovers what she is working on, she could be arrested for heresy. Or treason."

There was a long, drawn-out silence as both men considered that unpalatable possibility.

"Well," Dylan said finally, "I suppose that's all the more reason to figure out how to send you home in the proper time. In case you have to break your sister out of jail."

The intended joke fell decidedly flat.

Their spirits lowered by the peril Julianna Valderian insisted on courting, Starbuck and Dylan returned to the lab, where they worked for the next two hours. Starbuck was plotting new data into the computer, when he stood up so quickly the chair overturned.

"What's the matter?" Dylan asked, glancing up from his perusal of the lettuce-green printout.

"It's Charity. She is in trouble."

Dylan's brow furrowed. "I thought you couldn't read minds here on earth."

"I can read hers. And she needs a backup." He frowned as the ecumenical translator remained distressingly mute. "What's a *backup?*"

"Help." Dylan hit a few vital keys on the computer keyboard, saving the information while locking it safely from probing eyes. Then he was on his feet, as well. "Can you see where she is?"

Starbuck closed his eyes and concentrated on seeing through Charity's eyes. The image was vague, as if he were looking at it through a thick cloud of fog.

"There are a great many trees."

"Terrific," Dylan muttered. "That could be any place on the island."

"And a rocky shore with a thin strip of gray sand beach."

"At least that narrows it down a bit," Dylan said. "Keep trying."

"There is an old building. It has writing on the side."

Starbuck was finding it difficult to concentrate when his heart was pounding so hard. Since he'd never experienced absolute fear, not even his first day on the island when he'd thought he was going to die out in that blinding white blizzard, it took Starbuck a moment to recognize it.

"It reads Willow Fish Hatchery."

"Bingo." Dylan grabbed his coat and headed toward the door.

"Wait," Starbuck called after him. "She is not there."

"What?"

"She passed it on the way to her destination."

"Which is?" Aggravation roughened Dylan Prescott's tone.

"There is a lighthouse. And boats. And many bright buoys bobbing in a cove."

"Those mark the lobster traps," Dylan informed him. "She's at the wharf."

"Yes." Starbuck nodded. "And there's another building. The sign says The Stewed Clam. That's where she is."

"Oh, hell," Dylan muttered. "That's a harbor bar— no telling what kind of mess she's gotten herself into this time."

Starbuck remembered seeing a bunch of Janurian warriors get into an argument over an attractive Alean barmaid after imbibing too much Enos Dew. The ensuing fight had practically brought the place down.

"I will meet you there," he said, not wanting to waste the time it would take for Dylan's machine to maneuver over the snow-packed roads.

He crossed his arms, focused every atom of his being on his target and vanished from the laboratory.

CHARITY WAS DETERMINED not to let what had begun as a reasonably harmless fistfight turn into a brawl. Experience had taught her that a calm word, a quiet attitude, a low but authoritative voice could settle a situation with more efficiency than physical strength. Or firearms.

Even in a situation as potentially dangerous as this one. Two lobstermen were accusing another pair of raiding traps, which in this part of the country was on a par with horse stealing in the days of the Old West. The fact that all the parties involved had been drinking did not make matters any easier.

Charity was still trying to determine the facts of the case when the door opened and an all-too-familiar face appeared in a sudden flash of light.

Starbuck felt literally drained. The brief astro-projection had left him physically exhausted. Garnering much-needed strength, he glanced around, taking in the situation.

The waterfront tavern was much the same as the skyport taverns in his own galaxy. The air was thick with dense blue smoke, made even more unappealing by the smell of fish, sweat and a moldy odor that was a distinct contrast to the crisp salt air outside.

The bar shelves held only the basics—whiskey, vodka, tequila, rum and gin. The gin bottle was dusty, suggesting that it wasn't used all that often. Peanut shells and empty beer bottles littered the tops of tables.

Neon beer lights flickered, valiantly trying to cut through the cigarette smoke. Although three bare bulbs dangled from long cords, the bar was still dim.

The silver on the back of the mirror behind the bar had worn away, cracking the faces that looked back from it. Sections of brass bar rail were worn through. Above the bar was a painting of a well-formed woman clad in thigh-high black waders and a squall hat tilted at a rakish angle atop her sleek blond head.

Four men, wearing mackinaws and watch caps stood in the center of the room, hands curled into fists, faces twisted in anger. One man had a cut and bleeding lip, while his companion squinted through skin that was rapidly turning a bright blue. Starbuck realized that Charity had interrupted a brawl. She stood between the two pairs of men, looking very small and very vulnerable.

"What is the problem?" he asked, striding toward her.

"Nothing I can't handle," she said.

"None of your damn business," the man with the cut lip spat out at the same time.

"Well, whatever the problem, I'm sure we can settle it without bloodshed," Starbuck offered, ignoring the blistering glares directed his way.

"Starbuck—" Charity warned quietly.

He ignored her warning as he ignored the glares. "Logic can be a very useful tool."

"Who the hell is this guy?" the lobsterman with the darkening bruise slurred.

"My name is Bram Starbuck." Bran held out his hand. "And you are—?"

"Fed up." The taller of the two alleged poachers turned to leave, brushing Charity aside.

The sight of that man's beefy red hand touching her shoulder made something snap inside Starbuck. Although he'd never engaged in any sort of physical violence, something dark and primal, something decidedly un-Sarnian, surged through his veins. He struck out with a speed barely perceptible to the human eye.

The only proof he'd moved at all was the sight of the four men crumpling to the floor unconscious, one after the other, like falling timber.

As Starbuck stood over his vanquished opponents, he tried to remember a time when he'd felt so vividly, wonderfully alive and came up blank. He flexed his fingers with decided satisfaction.

He had studied Tal-shoyna for years, appreciating the way it stressed mental, rather than physical, control over an adversary. But there was a seldom discussed, darker side to the ancient martial arts method, as well— a movement that, if not carefully controlled, could break an opponent's neck quickly and cleanly.

Although there had been an instant when Starbuck had felt entirely capable of murder, he'd managed, at the last possible moment, to restrain the power surging through his fingertips.

"What the hell did you do?" Charity turned on him, her fists on her hips.

"They'll come to in time," Starbuck assured her. She seemed angry at him. Which was, of course, impossible. She should be grateful that he'd managed to rescue her with a minimum of violence. "Although their necks will be stiff for several days."

"You had no right to do that."

"You called for a backup."

"I did not!"

"Yes." He nodded. "You did."

There had been one moment when she'd wished that she could simply call for a backup in case things got a little sticky, the way she would have in California. But it had only been an instantaneous, fleeting mental wish.

She had no more time to think about it, because at that moment the men awoke with ragged groans, appearing a great deal more docile than they had earlier.

Charity was deciding what to do with them when the tavern door opened again, revealing Dylan. Behind him was Andy Mayfield, looking decidedly sheepish.

"I figured you might need a little help," Dylan greeted her. He glanced down at the men sitting peacefully on the floor. "But I guess you and Starbuck have everything under control."

"I had things under control," Charity snapped. "Before Starbuck interfered."

"*Interfered?*" His earlier satisfaction fading away like morning mist over her planet's seacoast, Starbuck stared at Charity in disbelief. He would have been no more surprised if she'd grown another head, like the aliens from planet Duality.

"Yes. Interfered." She shot him a hot, angry glare. "You're just lucky I'm not going to arrest you for obstruction of justice."

She turned to Andy. "Let's get these guys locked up so they can sleep it off. And then you and I—" she pointed at Starbuck "—are going to have a little talk."

Although he always enjoyed listening to Charity Prescott's musical cadence, Starbuck realized that the promised conversation would be anything but pleasant.

"Well," Dylan decided with false cheer, "now that everything's under control, I think I'll get back to work."

"You're afraid of your sister," Starbuck diagnosed.

"You bet your sweet bippy," Dylan agreed. "I've always made it a point to avoid angry women packing guns."

He patted Starbuck on the back and handed him some folded green bills. "Buy yourself some Dutch courage while you're waiting," he suggested. "And good luck. If you're still alive later this evening, I'll see you back at the lab."

With those ominous words ringing in Starbuck's ears, Dylan left.

Starbuck glanced around and realized that he was still the subject of a great deal of interest. Telling himself that he didn't really need a drink to fortify his courage, that he was merely thirsty, he went over to the bar.

"What'll it be?" the bartender asked.

He nearly asked for a flagon of Sirocco ale, then, remembering where he was, just in time, he said, "I'll have what he's having." He gestured toward the fisherman sitting on the stool beside him. The amber liquid certainly resembled ale.

"One draft, comin' up," the bartender agreed. He took down a glass and pulled a lever that dispensed the brew. Foam billowed over the top of the glass, ran down the side and went ignored. "That'll be a buck."

Having no idea of the denomination of the bills Dylan had handed him, Starbuck pulled one loose from the small stack and put it on the bar, hoping it would be sufficient. The bartender scooped up the money and returned more green bills to Starbuck.

"You're new around these parts."

"Yes." Starbuck took a tentative sip of the sparkling gold drink, felt the foam tickle his lips, then swallowed. The drink was smoother than the ale he was accustomed to drinking, more like water than a proper brew, and carried less of a kick.

"Since you know Dylan Prescott, you must be workin' out at that brain factory." His voice went up on the end of the statement, making it an obvious question.

"Yes," Starbuck said noncommittally, "I am working at the laboratory." He took another drink of beer, finding that the taste was improving.

"What on?"

"Excuse me?"

"What ya workin' on? Or is it classified?"

"Yes. It is classified."

"Ayuh, I figured as much," the bartender agreed without rancor. He began wiping the bar with a damp rag. "Most of the stuff theya doin' out there is pretty hush-hush. Which is why them space alien reports didn't much surprise me."

"Space aliens?"

"Little green men," the man next to Starbuck supplied. "A whole spaceship load of them landed in the town square and hightailed it into the woods."

"The ship was this shimmering blue light," the man on the other side of Starbuck divulged. "I was drivin' home and it damned near blinded me."

"It weren't blue at all," the first man argued. "It was white. And shaped like a cigar."

"I heard it was silver and shaped like a flying saucer," the bartender said. He took Starbuck's empty glass without asking, filled it to overflowing again and plucked a bill from the stack still lying on the bar.

"It was blue," the man to Starbuck's left insisted. "Filled with three-foot-tall green men with a single flashing eye in the middle of that forehead."

"You can't get anything right," the other man insisted. "They were seven-feet-tall men and were wearing Reynolds Wrap."

"Now where the hell is a spaceman gonna get his hands on Reynolds Wrap?" yet another man called out from a nearby table.

For the next twenty minutes, everyone in the bar was heatedly arguing about the aliens who were either here on a peace mission to warn of impending global destruction, planning to take over earth and enslave its population, or merely looking for brides to take home to their womanless planet.

Starbuck sat quietly, sipping his beer, waiting for Charity and wondering what they'd do if they knew the alien they were so enthusiastically arguing about was sitting in their midst.

"So what do you think?" the bartender asked him suddenly.

"About the aliens?"

"Ain't that what we've been talking about? What do you think they're doing here?"

Starbuck shrugged. "I hadn't realized that it had been proven that such aliens even existed."

"Oh, they exist, all right," the man beside him said. "I went to one of them UFO conferences in Bangor last month and saw the proof firsthand."

"Proof?"

"Photographs. Tons of them. Why, there was this one saucer landed at this farm in New York and after it left, the milk yield of each of his cows went from two and a half cans to only one. That was the bad news.

"But the farmer's wife had always had arthritis so bad she couldn't even hardly get out of bed. After that spaceship landed, the woman's arthritis disappeared and she took up square dancing."

"That's very interesting," Starbuck said politely.

"It's the truth."

"Well," Starbuck said, "if there are aliens, I'm sure they've come in peace."

"That's probably what the Poles said about the Germans just before World War II," one of the men muttered.

Starbuck was saved from any further discussion by Charity's arrival. One look at her tightly set face and flashing blue eyes made him decide that perhaps *saved* was not the correct term after all.

8

"IF YOU SO MUCH AS SAY one single word to me before we get to the house, I'll toss you back out into the snow," Charity warned him as they left the bar and headed for the Jeep.

From the barely reined fury in her tone, Starbuck decided it was not an idle threat. Reminding himself that women's thoughts were often unfathomable to men, and not wanting to upset her further, he held his tongue, watched the dazzling scenery flash by outside the window and tried to determine what had her so obviously out of sorts.

Starbuck understood the need for law-enforcement officials. The police on his planet existed to keep the offlanders in line. The average Sarnian was too passionless to even think about breaking the law: it would be illogical.

There were, of course, those whose biomental systems went awry, causing them to act in ways considered a threat to the group. But they were quickly taken away from society, and if the psychological mind-altering drugs did not solve the problem, they were deported to the moon Australiana, where they, and others like them, were doomed to spend the rest of their lives in exile.

Starbuck remembered when Julianna visited Australiana to study the life-style of its residents. When she returned, she shocked Starbuck by professing to admire the way each of the former Sarnians had, on his own initiative, taken on a task suited to his own individual abilities.

They were, she'd claimed, amazingly happy, for people who'd been banished from civilization. At the time, Starbuck had not given a great deal of thought to Julianna's remarks; now he was forced to wonder if perhaps his outwardly reserved sister had, at times, felt the same constraints of society as he often did.

That idea, like so many of the thoughts he'd been having lately, was a revelation.

Starbuck was given no more time to dwell on the idea that perhaps he'd misjudged Julianna. They'd reached Charity's house.

Still surrounded by an icy aura, she left the Jeep, slamming the driver's door behind her. Sighing, Starbuck followed.

They entered the house by the kitchen door. The fire was no longer burning, but the electric furnace kept the temperature at a comfortable seventy-four degrees. Starbuck watched as she hung her jacket on the peg by the door, then crossed the room and filled the teakettle.

"No coffee?" he asked with a casualness designed to mask his disappointment. He'd grown quite fond of the dark, vaguely bitter brew.

"The way I'm feeling, if I have any caffeine, I'd probably start throwing those knives at your head."

He followed her gesture to the black-handled knives thrust into a piece of wood beside the stove. "By all means, have the herbal tea."

She glared, looking as if she wished it were one of those knives. "Don't you dare patronize me."

"I wasn't patronizing you."

"Weren't you?"

The cat rose from the rug, stretched, then began demanding dinner. Muttering an oath, Charity obliged.

"No," Starbuck said when the cat had been fed, "I was in no way patronizing you."

She looked at him for a very long time, finally deciding to take his words at face value. "Good. Because I hate being patronized."

"May I ask why you are so angry?"

"Don't tell me you honestly don't know?"

"If I knew, I wouldn't ask," he said with easy logic. When she didn't immediately answer, he asked, "Are you in your cycle?"

"Why is it," she muttered fiercely, "that when a woman gets angry with a man—for very good reason, mind you—he tends to blame her behavior on PMS? No, I am not in my cycle. Not that it's any of your damn business," she tacked on.

"Under normal conditions, it would be true that it was not my business," he agreed. "But it is obvious that you are angry at me. So it is only logical that I would attempt to understand your uncharacteristically foul mood by eliminating all the possible reasons."

"There you go with that damn logic again," she flared furiously. "Was it logical for you to interfere with my work?"

Starbuck was momentarily distracted by the temper blazing in her eyes. She was, he decided, the most passionate individual he'd ever met. "You were in danger."

"I was not in danger. I had things under control, damn it!"

She stomped over to him, standing with her toes meeting his, and jabbed her finger into his chest. "I've already told you, Starbuck, before I came back to Castle Mountain, I'd arrested drug dealers and murderers and rapists who were a lot meaner and a great deal more deadly than those four drunken jerks.

"I had everything and everyone under control," she repeated hotly. "So why did you feel the damn need to interfere?"

"Interfere?" Starbuck felt himself losing his own temper, a temper he never knew he had. "You call rescuing you, at your request, interfering?"

"I didn't ask you for anything."

"You did, in your mind. And we both know it. You needed me, Charity Prescott. And I came."

"I don't need anyone," she flared.

"That's where you're wrong. You may be a police officer, but you can't change biology. You are only a woman."

"*Only* a woman?"

"Yes. A woman. Even you cannot deny that you are, physically, the weaker sex. And that being the case, it is the job of the stronger sex—men—to protect you. And since you are without a father or husband and your brother was detained, such duty fell to me."

"I am not anyone's damn duty!" His blatant male arrogance was infuriating. "You had no right to do what you did."

"On the contrary. I had every right."

"That's what you think."

"That is what I know," he shot back heatedly. "Because against all reason, I believe I am falling in love with you, Charity Prescott."

Charity had been about to blow sky-high. But those earth-shattering words, so simply stated, took the wind right out of her sails.

"That's impossible."

The teakettle began to whistle, its strident demand shattering the sudden quiet. Charity dragged it off the burner.

"Would you like some tea?" she asked in a voice that was not nearly as steady as she would have liked.

"I think you know what I'd like, Charity," Starbuck said softly.

Her back was to him. Charity closed her eyes and tried to garner strength. "It's too soon."

It crossed Starbuck's mind that he'd already been waiting centuries for this woman. "Yes, it probably is," he said instead. "And entirely unlike me. I am known for taking things slowly, for working out every possible consequence before I act."

"A typical scientist."

"Yes. But you are a far-from-typical woman, Charity. Which, I believe, is why I have been responding so uncharacteristically to your many charms these past three days."

Not to mention the nights. Her sensual dreams had invaded his mind, causing his body to ache and making sleep impossible.

Anxious for something to do, she poured the water into a mug, then dipped a tea bag into it, pretending vast interest in watching the liquid turn a light amber brown. "But you've practically ignored me ever since . . ."

"We kissed outside the lab that first morning."

"Yes." She hated letting him see how much his steely restraint had hurt her. "I thought you'd changed your mind. That you didn't find me attractive anymore."

"It's because I found you so appealing that I forced myself to back away from a potentially harmful situation."

"Oh." Charity considered that and felt better. "I guess I haven't exactly been myself, either," she admitted. "I've never been one to throw myself at a man I don't even know."

"I hoped that was the case."

Charity glanced back over her shoulder. "Ah, the male ego," she murmured with a faint smile. "How men can continue to insist that they're the stronger sex when they possess such fragile egos is beyond me."

The reluctant smile had warmed her eyes in a way that made Starbuck decide that fighting was the last thing he wanted to do with Charity.

As if she'd read his mind, she gave up on the tea and came to stand in front of him again. This time, instead of jabbing her finger against the front of his shirt, she pressed her palm against his chest.

"I want you," she admitted on a husky voice that curled around him like smoke. "And although it doesn't make a lick of sense, I think I wanted you before I even met you."

Was it only his imagination, or could he actually feel the warmth of her hand against his skin? Starbuck wondered. "When you were fantasizing about us together on Venice Beach."

"Yes. But I've spent a lot of time these past days thinking about it, Starbuck, and I've come to the reluctant conclusion that going to bed with you would probably be a major mistake."

"I won't hurt you, Charity."

That earned another faint smile. She lifted her hand to his cheek. "Yes, you will," she said softly. "Oh, you won't mean to," she said when he was inclined to argue. "But you will."

Her eyes were wide and blue and extremely vulnerable. Looking into them, Starbuck realized that what she said was true.

Even if Dylan hadn't explained about her generous heart, Starbuck would have realized that this was not the type of woman capable of having a brief, meaningless affair.

Charity Prescott was a warm and caring woman. She deserved a family, with a husband who loved her as deeply as she loved him, and children they could both love. That was something he couldn't give her.

And if he did give in to the impulses that seemed to be ruling his behavior whenever she was near, and took her to bed, what future could he offer her?

None, Starbuck considered bleakly. None at all.

"You're right." He backed slowly away. "It is obvious that you are a forever-after kind of woman."

Regret struck him like a fist. All his life he had been brought up to be totally honest. Never had the truth hurt so much.

"As much as I would like to offer you a future, I cannot give you what you need, Charity. What you deserve."

It took a major effort, but Charity managed to hide exactly how deeply his rejection stung. She felt, she considered, as if Starbuck had taken a whip to her heart.

So what were you expecting, kiddo? she asked herself. A poetic, bent-knee proposal from a man you've only known for three short days?

Yes. Unfortunately, irrationally, that's exactly what she'd been expecting.

"Well." She bit her lip and turned away. "A woman certainly can't accuse you of not being totally honest, Starbuck."

"It is the only way I know how to be."

There was something about the way he could be absolutely guileless, just at a moment when most men would, if not lie, at least shade the truth, that had Charity's heart softening toward him all over again.

She glanced up at the cuckoo clock on the wall. It would be dark soon. Night. A time for bed. The memory of waking up in this man's arms made her pulse run a little faster.

"What time do you have to be back at the brain factory?"

"Within the hour."

"So soon." She did not even try to conceal her disappointment.

"There is a great deal of work to be done, Charity," Starbuck said quietly. "And much of it must be done before the end of the solar flares."

The disappointment on her face was immediately replaced by curiosity. "Solar flares? Are you and Dylan studying their effects on emotions?"

"That's one of the things we are examining." He wondered what Charity would say if he told her what the main focus of their work was.

"It would be comforting to discover they're what's making everyone, including me, behave like a road company cast of *A Midsummer Night's Dream*."

Since his mother had the play on holotape, Starbuck was familiar with the Shakespearean sexual comedy of errors. He decided that her description was fairly accurate except for one important difference. His feelings for Charity had not been stimulated by any magical juice from any flower. They were, unnervingly, all too real.

"The flares may prove to be responsible for many things that have happened," he agreed. "But not my feelings for you."

She wondered why, if he honestly believed himself to be falling in love with her, he wasn't prepared to offer some semblance of commitment. A terrible thought occurred to her.

"Are you married?"

"Married?"

Starbuck was shocked that she'd even consider such a thing. If he were the type of self-indulgent man who could commit adultery, he definitely would have already experienced the pleasure of Charity in his bed.

"No. Of course I'm not married."

"Are you certain? After all, you still have amnesia, and it's possible—"

"I'm not married," he repeated firmly.

"Engaged?"

He'd already discovered his ability to hedge, or even to prevaricate, when necessary. But the plea in her soft blue eyes made Starbuck tell the truth when a lie would have sufficed.

"I seem to recall having an agreement with a woman."

"Oh." Charity's shoulders sagged. "Well, far be it from me to poach on another woman's territory."

"But she broke it off."

"Oh." It could have been his imagination, but Starbuck thought he saw a slight smile teasing at the corners of her lips.

He could have left it at that. Perhaps he even should have left it at that. But in all fairness, he couldn't. "I had hoped to change her mind."

The slight smile faded, a shadow moved across her lovely eyes. "Well. I'm sure you will. I can't imagine you not succeeding in anything you wanted to do," she said flatly.

He wanted to tell Charity that meeting her had made him question everything about his life, including Sela. He longed to take her in his arms and experience what he suspected would be a mindblinding experience. He wished he could stay here, with her, forever.

"My Grandmother Prescott had a saying," Charity said quietly. "If wishes were horses, beggars would ride."

He was looking at her. Looking hard, looking deep. Had his control slipped again, making him speak out loud? Or had she read his mind?

"It is as if we were bonded in some essential way," he said slowly. "You called for me—"

"I did not."

He waved away her protest with his hand. "You called for me," he repeated stubbornly. "And I came. And now, although everyone knows that it's impossible, you are in my mind, reading my thoughts."

"I wasn't reading your mind."

"Then how do you explain knowing what I was thinking? What I was wishing?"

"I was reading your face," Charity said. "You have a very expressive face, Starbuck."

"I do?"

That came as a surprise. It was something he would have to work on when he returned to Sarnia. Experiencing emotions was bad enough; letting others know he was feeling them would further diminish his credibility in the scientific community.

Charity laughed as she watched the surprise in his eyes be replaced by first alarm, then resolve. He was so open, this man she feared she was falling in love with. So honest. And so very different from Steven. For her former husband, lying and cheating had been much the same as breathing. He did it regularly and without any conscious thought.

"Now it is you who has the expressive face," Starbuck murmured. He traced her frowning lips with his thumb. "I hope I am not the one who caused that scowl."

His light touch was leaving sparks on her skin. Why was it that although they both knew there was no future in this relationship, although they both continued to swear not to continue it, they couldn't seem to stop touching each other?

"No. I was thinking of someone else."

"The man who hurt you."

"I don't want to talk about Steven," she insisted, backing away both figuratively and emotionally. "I don't want to think about him."

She'd let her heart rule her head once in her life. After she'd survived that debacle, she had sworn never to give her heart to another man. And here she was about to make the same mistake.

Starbuck nodded. "I can understand how such a subject could be painful to you."

"Not painful," Charity flared. "It just makes me angrier than hell."

Starbuck had already decided that there was no more exciting sight than the flare of temper in Charity's blue eyes. Once again he found himself wanting her. Once again he reminded himself that he dare not.

Charity watched the emotions move in waves across his face again. Passion, desire, resolve. And then the walls went up again and she found herself standing on the other side, out in the cold. Bram Starbuck was not an easy man to know. He would not be an easy man to love.

The cuckoo clock struck the hour, the strident bird coming out of its wooden house to shatter an expectant silence that was growing more and more dangerous by the moment.

It crossed Starbuck's mind that the bird clock could have been a metaphor for many of the terrans he'd met during his brief stay: strange, funny, totally illogical and oddly appealing.

"You'd better be getting back to the brain factory."

"Yes." Starbuck's own tone was as reluctant as hers.

"Why don't you take the Jeep? I won't be going out."

"Thank you." He nodded. "You're very generous."

"I've been told that's my problem."

He gave her another of his long, thoughtful looks. "Perhaps," he agreed finally. "But it's also one of your most endearing charms."

Unable to resist the lure of those soft pink lips, he caught her chin in his fingers and kissed her, a quick, nonthreatening brush of lips. It still left him shaken. Starbuck dropped his hands to his sides and stepped back.

"Static electricity," Charity managed to suggest through lips that burned from his touch. "The rug has a nylon backing."

"That's undoubtedly it," Starbuck agreed, anxious, desperate to grab on to some scientific reason for yet another physically riveting response. At the same time, he couldn't help noticing that once again they were thinking the same thought.

"Dylan will be wondering what happened to me."

"If my brother is working, an earthquake could happen right beneath his desk and unless his beloved computer fell into it, he wouldn't even notice," Charity said dryly.

Starbuck smiled. "Julianna has been known to say much the same thing about me."

"Julianna's your sister," Charity remembered. "The something-anthropologist."

"Xenoanthropologist."

"That's right. I'd like to meet her. It sounds as if we have a lot in common."

Actually, Starbuck had never met two more dissimilar women. But he loved them both, each in a different way.

"And have the two of you discussing me like a frozen slide under a microscope?" he asked with mock horror. "I know you, Charity Prescott. Within five minutes of meeting Julianna, you would have her revealing all my secrets."

"Do you have all that many secrets, Starbuck?" Charity asked on a quick, unsteady laugh that unwillingly revealed that it was not a very casual question.

"Enough," Starbuck said truthfully. When she looked inclined to delve deeper, he said, "I really must go."

"Sure." Charity shrugged with feigned nonchalance as she handed him the Jeep keys. "Drive carefully."

"I will do my best not to crash your machi—your Jeep," he corrected quickly.

Starbuck looked up at the clock and damned his new enemy—time. Although he knew he should be spending every waking hour in the laboratory, he wanted to savor whatever little bit of time he had left on Earth with Charity.

"Maybe, if you finish up at a reasonable hour," Charity suggested, "we could have a late supper."

Again she seemed able to read his mind with an alacrity that was both startling and disturbing. "I'd like that. But I wouldn't want you to go to the trouble of cooking."

She laughed at that. "I have no intention of putting your life at risk like that, Starbuck. I thought I might heat up a frozen pizza."

"Perfect." Charity and pizza. Now that was truly nirvana.

He bent his head and brushed his lips lightly, briefly, against hers. That one kiss led to another, then another, until they were both breathless.

Finally, reluctantly, giving in to his obligations, Starbuck left the house. Engrossed as he was in thoughts of Charity, Starbuck failed to see the solitary figure hidden in the grove of snow-draped pine trees, watching the house with unwavering intensity.

9

As if by mutual, unspoken consent, Starbuck and Charity spent the next two weeks struggling to avoid temptation. And although it was by no means an easy task, their steadfast refusal to allow any overt physical intimacy resulted in an emotional intimacy that ran stronger and deeper than the chemistry that had raged between them from the beginning.

Gradually, day by day, they grew increasingly closer. Charity was surprised at how easily Starbuck fit into the routine of her life. Over morning coffee and late-night hot chocolate, she discovered that Starbuck was a great deal like her brother—startlingly brilliant, impossibly driven, yet possessing a warm and caring heart.

And even as she reminded herself that he'd promised her no future—on the contrary, he'd been quite specific about his inability to offer her any type of long-term commitment—her unruly heart seemed determined to overrule her cautious head. Her feelings for him became hopelessly tangled, frustratingly complicated.

But whenever she'd try to sort them out, the bottom line was always the same—despite every vestige of common Yankee sense she possessed, she was falling deeper in love with the man with each passing day.

While Charity struggled with her turmoiled emotions, Starbuck found himself no less affected. Deep-seated needs he hadn't even known he possessed were growing inside him—needs that were battering away at the barricades he was trying so hard to maintain between them. Despite his best efforts to avoid emotional entanglements, Charity had made a difference in his life. A difference he could no longer ignore.

"What are you doing tonight?" she asked one morning as they drank their coffee and read the *Yankee Observer* at the kitchen table.

Starbuck shrugged. "I thought I'd run a new program." He refrained from telling her that he and Dylan had come up with a hypothesis regarding his trip home. A trip, that, if Dylan's projections were correct, would be two short days away. "Why?"

"I don't know if you've heard about it, locked up in the brain factory, but Winterfest begins tonight."

"I believe Vanessa mentioned something about that," Starbuck murmured obliquely. Actually she'd invited him to accompany her to the annual festivities.

"I'll just bet she did."

Starbuck framed her frowning face between his palms. Her hair, backlit by the fire, resembled a coppery halo. "I should have asked you to attend the festival with me."

She absolutely refused to meet his warm gaze. "Don't do me any favors."

"It is you who will be doing me a favor, Charity. I've never experienced a Winterfest." Actually, until he'd arrived in Maine, he'd never experienced snow or ice. "I can't think of anything I'd rather do than attend with you."

"You don't have to work late?"

"Work can wait." Starbuck could not believe he had actually said that. "I'd rather be with you."

Charity smiled. "If we leave here by six, we'll be at the square in time for dinner. You haven't tasted anything until you've tasted a genuine Maine lobster."

"Six, it is." The problem would be keeping his mind on his work for the next ten hours.

UNDAUNTED BY the frigid elements, it appeared that all the residents of Castle Mountain Island had turned out for the first night of the three-day Winterfest.

Mother Nature had cooperated by bestowing a cold, clear night for the festivities. The black velvet sky was spangled with glittering stars. The trees on Main Street had been sprayed with water that had frozen to a brilliant crystalline ice. In addition, they'd strung fairy lights through the bare branches. In the center of the town square was a towering white castle, carved from blocks of ice and, like the trees, draped in tiny white lights.

"Oh!" Charity breathed. "Isn't it lovely?"

"Absolutely," Starbuck agreed. But he wasn't looking at the light-adorned ice castle. He was looking at her.

Color rose in her cheeks. "If you keep looking at me that way," she complained, "we'll never make it to dinner."

As delicious as he suspected Maine's famous lobster to be, Starbuck knew the taste would never surpass the flavor of her sweet lips.

"Would you stop that," she said when he told her exactly what he was thinking. "Everyone is already looking at us. In another minute, they'll have us headed down the aisle."

Starbuck found that idea strangely, eminently appealing. He put his arm around her shoulder. "Lobster it is," he said with a bland smile designed to keep that dangerous thought to himself. "Lead the way."

The lobster, served with hot, dripping butter, was everything Charity had promised. And more. Starbuck wondered if terrans knew how fortunate they were to be privy to such a wonderful variety of rich and delicious foods.

The community dinner, held in the town hall, was a potluck, designed to raise much-needed funds for the charity food bank that had been depleted by recent holiday demands. Many of the women in the town appeared to be determined to outdo each other, arriving with dishes designed to tempt the palate.

Charity, not trusting her culinary skills, had purchased a cake from a local bakery. When she informed Starbuck that the rich concoction had been named Death By Chocolate, he decided that it wouldn't be such a bad way to go.

And that was just the beginning. As they toured the display of ice sculptures created by citizens turned annual artists, oohing and aahing over a towering Statue of Liberty, admiring a delicately carved fox, running gloved hands over the antlers of a full-size ice moose, Starbuck was treated to a dazzling plethora of taste treats. Chunks of creamy chocolate fudge, cups of hot spiced apple cider and dark red mulled wine, crisp maple sugar cookies, roasted chestnuts.

"I may never eat again," he complained after devouring a tub of hot buttered popcorn that brought back memories of his long-ago trip to Disneyland.

"That's what you say now," she said. "Just wait until tomorrow evening. That's when they have the pie bake-off."

Despite the fact that his stomach felt as if it were going to burst, when she started naming the variety of pies entered by local bakers, Starbuck's mouth began to water.

As he met more and more of Castle Mountain's residents, Starbuck felt a bonding, a sense of community that he had never experienced on Sarnia. For not the first time since his arrival in the isolated island village, he found himself wishing that he could remain in Castle Mountain. With Charity.

But, whenever he felt himself wavering, Starbuck reminded himself of how much he had to teach his scientific community back on Sarnia. What would have happened if Copernicus and all the others who followed him had kept their discoveries to themselves?

A white horse clopped by, pulling behind it an old-fashioned sleigh. "Come for a ride with me?" Charity invited.

"Anywhere," Starbuck answered promptly.

Soon they were bundled up in the back of the sleigh, blankets wrapped tightly around them. The night was icy cold, the sky crystal clear. As the sleigh's runners clicked against the crunchy snow and the bells on the horse's harness jingled merrily, Starbuck drew her close. Unprotesting, Charity rested her head on his shoulder and sighed, that soft, pleased breath more eloquent than any words.

Her scent teased as they rode through the night. The ride was over all too soon. Starbuck was just about to suggest they take another, when her pager stuffed away in her parka pocket sounded.

This time her sigh was one of resignation. "I'd better answer it," she apologized.

Starbuck bit back his frustration and gave her a smile. "Of course."

Starbuck accompanied her to the police station and waited while she dialed the number that had appeared on her pager. "Damn." She dragged her hand through her hair, ruffling the bright strands. "I'll be right there." She reached into a drawer and pulled out her service revolver.

"What are you doing?"

"Dan Olson got drunk and began arguing with his wife," she said. "From what I could tell, things were getting a little out of hand when the Olsons' teenage son came home and discovered that Dan had hit Eileen. According to their neighbor, who just called to report the fight, the kid is holding his father at gunpoint."

A hormone-driven teenage boy, even on Sarnia, was capable of turbulent, dangerous emotions. A terran teenager with a gun could be especially deadly.

"Let Andy take this call."

Charity stared up at him. "Why?"

"Because it's dangerous, damn it."

"It's also my job."

Concern made him rash. "That's ridiculous."

Her face closed as she encased herself in enough ice to surround the planet Algor. "What's ridiculous is your attitude. We're wasting time. I'll be back in a while."

"If you think I'm letting you face some wired-up kid with a weapon alone, you're crazy."

Little white lines framed her lips. "This is my work, Starbuck. It's who I am."

"It's what, against all that is reasonable, you *do*, damn it," Starbuck argued. "Not who you *are*."

She gave him a long, unfathomable look. "You're wrong. Because it's both."

Then she turned and headed toward the door.

Starbuck followed on her heels. "I'm coming with you."

"I don't want you to."

"Tough." The back-and-forth motion of his jaw suggested Starbuck was grinding his teeth. "You can try and stop me. But I have to warn you, Officer, you're going to have to use that weapon to do it."

She looked up at him, her gaze sweeping over his rigidly set features. "You have to promise not to interfere."

"Damn it, Charity—"

"Promise."

Silently he raved his way through every Sarnian curse he knew. And then he started in on a few of the more pungent outlander oaths. But he said, "All right."

She gave him one more quick study, then, apparently reminding herself that he never lied, said, "Fine. Let's go."

They drove in silence through the dark, the Jeep's headlights cutting a yellow swathe through the night. There had been times during the past weeks that their silences had been companionable. This one was not.

In contrast to that first night, when the raging blizzard had forced her to drive with extreme caution, Charity kept her foot on the gas pedal all the way out of town. Twice she nearly skidded on a patch of ice, twice she deftly corrected. Once again, Starbuck admired her driving skill. Although he'd throw himself into a snowdrift before admitting it, the first time he'd borrowed her vehicle, he'd found even shifting gears baffling.

Less than five minutes later, she pulled off the main road and headed down a washboard-rough frozen dirt trail.

"I want you to stay in the Jeep," she said as she pulled up in front of a weather-beaten building.

"I only agreed not to interfere," Starbuck reminded her. "I never said I'd stay in the truck."

"Are you always this stubborn?" she flared.

"Always."

Muttering an oath, she flung open the driver's door, jumped down from the front seat and began stomping through the snow. After countering with another string of archaic Sarnian curses, Starbuck followed.

The scene in the modest but tidy living room was definitely not one of family harmony. A woman Starbuck judged to be in her late thirties or early forties was frozen beside a saggy sofa. Her sable hair was streaked with threads of gray, her thin lips, caught between her teeth, were unadorned with any flattering color. A bruise stained her cheek, darkening purple against a stark-white complexion. She looked worn and tired and scared.

In contrast, her husband's dark eyes flashed with a black malevolence when Charity and Starbuck entered the house.

"Damn it, this isn't any of your business, Charity Prescott." The growl in Dan Olson's voice would have done justice to an Australianan rock tiger.

"Sorry, Dan, but I'm afraid it is." She turned calmly to the boy, whose face—as white as his mother's—was blotchy with scarlet anger. "Eric, this isn't a very good idea."

"The bastard hit Mom." Eric Olson was trembling so much that the barrel of the shotgun began to shake. But he kept it pointed directly at his father.

"Damn it, it was an accident," Dan Olson insisted hotly. Not one person in the room believed him.

"I'm going to make damn sure there aren't any more *accidents*." Eric's young voice, still in the process of changing, cracked.

"I understand why you're upset, Eric." Charity's voice was as calm as a tranquil sea, as smooth as glass. "I also think any mother would be proud to have such a protective son."

She paused a heartbeat of a second, watching the barrel of the gun lower infinitesimally. "But think how your mother would feel if she had to spend the next twenty-five years visiting you in prison."

"I just want things to be the way they used to be," Eric complained.

"I know." Charity started toward him. "Times have been rough on a lot of people. Which is why families have to stand together now, more than ever."

The hands that held the gun were shaking. "He shouldn't have hit her."

"It was an accident," Dan Olson insisted. The embarrassed red flush rising from his collar suggested otherwise.

"An accident," Eileen seconded her husband's assertion. Tears streaked down her cheeks, leaving mascara-darkened tracks.

Eric looked with disbelief at his mother. "How can you stick up for him?" His shoulders sagged, his arms lowered. The barrel was now pointing at the floor. But the danger, Charity knew from past experience, was far from over.

"One thing I've discovered about life, Eric," she advised, "is that it tends to get sticky from time to time." There was a relieved sigh from every adult in the room as she took the shotgun from the boy. "And sometimes it's unfair. But violence is never the answer."

"Try telling that to him," Eric blazed with a renewed flare of anger.

"That's exactly what I intend to do." Charity turned to Starbuck. "Would you take Eric for a walk to help him work off some of his excess energy while I talk with Dan and Eileen?"

"Sure." Not knowing what to say but trusting that Charity had the matter well in hand, Starbuck threw his arm around the boy's shoulder. "Come on, Eric," he invited. "I caught a glimpse of a beaver dam on your pond when we drove by. Why don't we see if we can catch a glimpse of any activity?"

As soon as they were gone, Charity turned her not inconsiderable persuasion skills on his parents. By the time Starbuck and Eric had returned to the house twenty minutes later, Dan had agreed to spend the night at his brother's house, in lieu of being locked in Castle Mountain's single jail cell, and both adults had agreed to begin family counseling.

Knowing their tenuous financial situation, Charity had promised to help them with the red tape necessary to enter a program for low-income families.

As Charity drove the Jeep back down the washboard road, both remained lost in their own thoughts.

"I'm impressed," Starbuck said finally, when they pulled up in front of Charity's house.

His quiet compliment should not have given her so much pleasure. But it did. "Thanks."

"When we arrived, I took one look at that boy's face and felt certain that there would be violence. But you managed to forestall it without even drawing your own weapon."

Her casual shrug, as she twisted the key, turning off the ignition, belied the pleasure his words instilled. "That would have only created a worse problem. Contrary to what you see on television, cops would rather use their mouths than their guns."

She looked out the windshield at the softly falling snow and turned thoughtful. "When I first graduated from the police academy, I honestly believed that my job was to solve all society's problems."

"A herculean, and highly improbable task."

"I couldn't have put it better myself," Charity agreed. "Anyway, eventually, I realized that life wasn't neatly black-and-white. That mostly it was varying shades of muddy gray. And that my job would be coming up with a temporary solution for a long-term problem."

"I'm not certain I understand."

"Most of the problems cops encounter are started by someone or something else. And ultimately, they'll be finished by someone else. Hopefully, in the Olsons' case, a good counselor coupled with an upturn in the economy will ease some of the tension the family's been under. Meanwhile, we get the parts in-between."

"The Olsons were fortunate to have you taking care of the in-between. I think you are a very good police officer, Charity Prescott."

"High praise indeed, from a professed male chauvinist." Charity rewarded him with a smile. "Perhaps there's hope for you, after all, Starbuck."

Their eyes met. "Charity—" Starbuck ran the back of his hand down her cheek and felt her tremble.

"Yes." She closed her eyes and allowed emotions too long denied to surge through her. When she opened her eyes again, her gaze was frank and open. "I want to make love with you, Starbuck," she said in a voice that was as thick as honey and as warm as a late-summer sun.

It was what he'd been wanting from the beginning. Torn between honor and need, Starbuck hesitated. During that fleeting vacillation, the cellular phone rang, shattering the moment.

Slanting him an apologetic glance, Charity scooped it up. "Police department. Oh, Dylan." Her tone was anything but welcoming. "Yes, he's right here." She handed the phone to Starbuck. "It's for you."

Frowning, Starbuck listened to Dylan's excited voice. And knew that fate had just intervened.

"He believes he's made a breakthrough," Starbuck answered Charity's questioning look.

That much was true. He refrained from mentioning that someone had tried to break into the computer files.

"So you need to go to the lab."

Stay. Go. He'd never been more torn.

Taking pity on him, Charity pressed her fingers against his tightly set lips. "Go to the brain factory," she advised. "There'll be another time."

Had there ever been a woman like this one? Starbuck wondered. "I won't be long," he promised.

Disappointed but determined not to show it, Charity forced a smile. "I'll be waiting."

THE FOLLOWING DAY dawned crisp and clear and cold. Charity was sitting at the kitchen table, after having drunk too many cups of coffee, waiting for Starbuck to return.

He'd been gone all night. Frustrated, lonely and needing to work off her anxiety, she pulled on her hooded parka and left the house. Perhaps some exercise in the fresh air would clear her head. It was, she mused as she trod through the now-crunchy frozen snow, as if Starbuck possessed the ability to fog her mind.

She couldn't figure him out. It was obvious that he cared for her. Just as it was obvious that he'd tried very hard not to care. Charity knew that the man she'd fallen in love with was hiding something. Although he appeared incapable of telling a lie, there was something Starbuck wasn't saying. Something important.

Determined to drive to the lab and settle matters once and for all, she turned around and headed back toward the house. Caught up in her tumultuous thoughts, she failed to see the figure emerge from behind a towering pine tree. Neither did she see the tree limb come crashing down on her head.

10

STARBUCK FOUND HER like that, crumpled like a dead robin in the snow. As he gathered her into his arms, for the first time in his life, he understood the sheer force of a fury that could drive a man to murder.

"Charity."

His gloved hands brushed over her face, brushing off the snow. Her cheeks were chapped to the dark pink color of an Australianan moonrise.

"Sweetheart, wake up."

Her lashes were a tawny fringe against those too-pink cheeks. Her lips were softly parted. It was only the slow steady breath he felt slipping between those lips that kept Starbuck from giving in to the panic he was feeling.

She wasn't dead. No thanks to him. Because although the thought was untenable, Starbuck suspected that whoever had attacked Charity had been after his work.

"Charity, please, you have to wake up."

Her lids fluttered open. "Starbuck?" Smiling vaguely, she lifted a hand to his face. "You came back."

"I told you I would." Last night, damn it. He'd promised to return hours ago, but like a Haldon-headed idiot, he'd allowed himself to get immersed in Dylan's mystery and had let the time slip away from him.

His anger at himself for leaving Charity alone for those long hours, was steamrollered by an icy fear that

if he'd lingered at the lab for only a few more minutes . . .

No! The thought was unpalatable. Shaking off the
image of a lifeless Charity, he gathered her into his
arms, intending to carry her back to the house.

But although the gash on her head was readily ap-
parent, Charity proved that her mind had not been affected. "How did you get here?" she asked suddenly.

"How do you think? When I returned to the house
and found you missing, I walked out here, looking for
you." It was one of the few out-and-out lies he'd told
her. In truth, when he'd seen her, in his mind's eye, lying in the snow, he'd transported himself to her side by
telekinesis.

"But the only tracks in the snow are mine. Except for
those," she said, pointing out another pair that disappeared into the trees. She could see those same tracks
coming this way. Since they were too small to belong
to Starbuck, she realized they'd been left by whoever it
was that had struck her.

Charity stared around at the undisturbed snow, then
up at Starbuck.

"I think," she said, "that it's time we had a long talk."

As he carried her back to the house, Charity was
trying not to believe what her very own eyes were telling her.

Starbuck, too, was attempting to figure out how to
explain that he was a half human, half Sarnian space
traveler who'd accidentally gotten a little off course
while crossing subspace due to solar flares and landed
on the wrong edge of the continent two hundred years
before schedule.

Would she believe him? The chances were undoubtedly the same as her believing in those little green men who'd been reported, he decided grimly.

"I'll put on a fresh pot of coffee," he said when they entered the house, stamping snow off his feet.

"You can put me down now," she said. "And I have a feeling this is probably going to call for something stronger than coffee."

"I think you're right."

She shook her head, still unable to believe what she was thinking. There was some logical, rational reason for all this, Charity knew. All she had to do was figure it out.

Perhaps, her desperate mind considered, she was merely dreaming. Eager to try anything, Charity pinched herself. Hard.

"Why did you do that?"

"I was hoping that I was dreaming."

"I'm afraid this is not a dream, Charity." His deep voice was more solemn than she'd ever heard it. That, along with the regret in his eyes, frightened her.

"Yeah. I'd already come to that conclusion all by myself." Charity went into the adjoining living room. Starbuck followed, running into her when she came to an abrupt halt.

"Charity?" A chill raced up his spine. "What's wrong?"

"It's Dylan's computer," she murmured. "Someone's been using it." She walked across the room and ran her fingers over the keyboard. The disk-drive door was open. She flicked the black tab down, effectively closing the door. "You know, I thought I heard someone in here that first night you were here."

A memory flooded into his mind. He remembered knowing that Charity was in danger and thinking that he must save her, but his rebellious, weakened body had refused to cooperate.

"You searched the room and found nothing."

"That's right." She was not as surprised as she might have once been that he knew what she'd been doing while he was supposed to be unconscious. "But finally I decided that it must have been my imagination playing tricks on me."

"Because of all the alleged spaceship sightings."

"I suppose they had something to do with it," she admitted reluctantly.

"Surely you don't think that little green men have been infiltrating themselves into Dylan's top-secret study?"

"No." She laughed at that. "Not even my imagination is that active. But Dylan's been real hush-hush about this project. It wouldn't surprise me to learn that someone was after it."

That was, unfortunately, the same conclusion Starbuck had come to. Especially since Dylan had been right about someone trying to crack the security code at the lab. Apparently, he decided, when the intruder failed to gain entrance to the mainframe, he'd broken into Charity's home, hoping that Dylan might have left the PC unsecured.

"Whoever was using his computer is undoubtedly the same person who hit you on the head."

"It would seem so," Charity agreed. "And I'd call the police, but unfortunately, I am the police."

She rubbed the back of her head where a headache was beginning to throb and was surprised when she took her hand away and saw the red stain on her fingers.

"You're bleeding!"

Starbuck, who had managed to live thirty years without seeing blood of any kind, either Sarnian green or human red, felt suddenly faint at the sight. But the idea that it was Charity's blood staining her delicate hand caused a rush of pure fury that burned away his dizziness.

"It's just a flesh wound," she said with a crooked smile.

She was brave. Starbuck would give her that. He watched the color fade from her face, saw the pain in her eyes and knew that she would refuse to admit she was hurting.

"That is probably the case," he agreed. "But we should clean it so it does not become infected."

She shook her head, wishing she hadn't when huge boulders began rattling around inside. "We need to talk."

"We will talk later. Right now we need to tend to your injury. Where is your disinfectant?"

"In the bathroom. Men," she huffed. "You're all so damn bossy."

"And women are all so frustratingly stubborn." Before she could discern his plan, he'd scooped her up in his arms again and was marching toward the fragrant room with the flowered walls.

"Starbuck," Charity protested, "I'm perfectly capable of walking a few feet by myself."

"You are pale. I don't want you to faint."

"That's ridiculous. I never faint." She combed frustrated hands through her hair, surprised when they came away with even more blood.

He closed the lid, then sat her down onto the commode. Was it her imagination, or had the purple flowers on the wall begun to dance?

"Why, my rookie year I was on patrol with this veteran cop. He had nineteen years under his belt and was six months away from retirement when we got a call about a woman in labor stuck in traffic on the San Diego Freeway."

Charity blinked. It wasn't her imagination, she decided. The flowers were dancing. And spinning. And spinning. She closed her eyes.

"My partner told me to let him handle everything. But as soon as he saw the baby's head coming out, this big, strong, two-hundred-pound male passed out."

The floor beneath the commode tilted. "I ended up delivering the baby all by myself. It was a girl. Eight pounds, three ounces. They named her..."

Charity slumped forward and were it not for Starbuck catching her, she would have slid onto the fluffy white rug.

IT WAS SUMMER. The sun was the color of rich, freshly churned butter. It warmed her face as she lay on her back in a field of purple and pink wildflowers. Her eyes were closed and Charity was luxuriating in the heady pleasure of a day spent doing nothing.

She heard the footfalls approaching and knew instinctively who it was.

"I've been looking for you." The deep voice was wonderfully familiar.

It took a mighty effort, she felt so wonderfully lethargic, but Charity managed, finally, to open her eyes.

"And I've been waiting for you," she said, looking up at the man who appeared little more than a silhouette surrounded by bright yellow rays of sunshine.

She couldn't see his face, but she knew what he looked like. His hair would be dark, black as a crow's wing. And his eyes would be dark, as well, like obsidian, only so much softer. Particularly when they looked at her.

He knelt beside her and she saw that she was right. Not questioning how or why he'd come, she lifted a hand to his dark cheek.

"I've been waiting," she repeated in a soft, breathless voice. "All of my life."

"What a coincidence," he murmured. Taking hold of her hand, he turned his head, pressed a kiss against her palm and made her flesh burn. "Since I've been looking for you all of my life."

Destiny had brought them together. And now there was no need for preliminaries. His clever hands undressed her, long dark fingers maneuvering the buttons of her sundress with an ease she would have expected from a man who'd played the starring roles in her romantic fantasies for years.

The flowered cotton dress disappeared as if by magic, leaving her clad in a peach teddy trimmed in ivory lace. "You are so lovely." He ran a slow, tantalizing finger along the lace at the bodice of the teddy, his touch burning her so she wondered why the silk and lace hadn't gone up in flames.

"I'm too fat." For some horrid reason she felt obliged to tell the truth. "I need to lose ten pounds."

"That's ridiculous." His hands skimmed over her. "You're just right." He cupped her breast, caressing it with a tender touch that left her aching. When he brushed his thumb over her silk-clad nipple, Charity felt a delicious tug of expectation between her thighs.

"Everywhere you have a curve, my sweet Charity—" his mouth dampened first the silken bodice, then the skin beneath it "—I have a hollow."

Stretching out beside her, he brought her against him. "See?" His lips nuzzled at her ear, her neck. "We are a perfect fit."

It seemed to be true. Her body, which she'd always considered too round, fit against his as if it were one of two perfect parts of a puzzle.

"A perfect fit," she agreed, lifting her arms around his neck. Her body seemed gloriously light. Free. A sweet pleasure flowed through her like summer sunshine.

A soft breeze shimmied across the meadow, causing the blossoms to bob their purple heads. Hummingbirds, their slender throats gleaming like emeralds, flittered here and there, gathering up the fragrant nectar with their long slender beaks, in much the same way her fantasy man was kissing her now.

His lips were drinking from hers as if he would never get enough of her taste. Her lips parted on a soft sigh, offering everything she was. Everything she would ever be.

The sun seemed trapped in her skin, warming it all the way to the bone; the air was redolent with the sweet scents of flowers and the salt tang of the sea. And the unmistakable scent of desire.

His arms tightened around her, fitting her to his body so tightly that the breeze couldn't come between them. Their clothes were gone, as if seared away by the rising heat of their desire, and as her hands explored the rippling muscles of his back, she was rewarded by a low, masculine moan.

She heard her name vibrating against her breast, tasted it when he returned his mouth to hers. His chest was covered with an arrowing of crisp dark hair that rubbed against her taut, ultrasensitive nipples and made them ache.

Charity had never felt so much a prisoner of her emotions. Never had she felt so free. Laughing softly, she pulled away from his embrace. Kneeling beside him in the bed of flowers, she moved her hands over his sun-dappled body, skimming, caressing, kneading, arousing.

She plucked a purple blossom and trailed it over his shoulders, down his chest, over his stomach. She drew it up first one hair-roughened thigh and then the other, fascinated by the way his muscles clenched beneath his dark flesh.

So much man, she considered headily. And he was hers. All hers.

They could have been the only two people in the universe. The first man and woman. Or the last. Like Eve, she tempted. Like Adam, he succumbed.

In that bright light of a summer day, dark secrets as old as time were revealed. There was no need to hurry; anticipation only added to the pleasure. Time, for this suspended moment, stood gloriously still.

Through the golden mists, she heard him say her name. *Charity.* All his feelings for her, all the love, vibrated in that single word. It sounded like a poem. Or a prayer. It sounded wonderful.

"CHARITY." Starbuck ran the cool cloth over her forehead, down her cheeks, across her closed lids. "Sweetheart, please wake up. You're frightening me."

The dream was fading, back into the mists of her mind. Poised on the edge of fulfillment, Charity struggled against the rising consciousness.

"Charity." There was a low, inarticulate oath. "I'm going to call a doctor."

"No." The fantasy disintegrated like fog over the tops of the trees, leaving her frustrated and unsatisfied. "I'm all right."

"Are you sure?"

"Yes."

Charity opened her eyes and looked right into Starbuck's dark gaze. She was no longer in the bathroom. Instead, she was lying atop of her Grandmother Prescott's wildflower quilt. Starbuck was sitting on the edge of the bed, concern etched all over his handsome features.

"I was dreaming about you."

Starbuck ran the back of his hand down her still-pale cheek. "I hope that explains the smile."

"It was a very good dream," she admitted. "It was summer and we were lying—"

"In a field of wildflowers. And you told me that you've been waiting for me all your life. And I told you that I'd been looking for you all my life."

"Yes."

His words should have surprised her. Two weeks ago, she wouldn't have believed it possible for two people to be so in tune with each other. But two weeks ago, she hadn't met Starbuck.

"You were reading my mind, weren't you?"

"Yes. And I owe you an apology for that, but I find that I can't sincerely express regret. Since that was the moment when I realized it was true."

His gaze moved lovingly over her face, lingering on her lips. "I have been searching for you all my life. . . .

"It wasn't the solar flares that brought me here. It was destiny. And you." He combed his fingers through her hair, sifting the coppery strands between his fingers, watching them shimmer in the muted glow of the lamplight. "Because you are my destiny, Charity Prescott."

And he was hers. It sounded so perfect. So wonderfully, magically perfect. But experience had taught Charity that magic, while appealing, was merely cleverly staged illusion.

"If that's true, why do you look as if there's something terribly wrong? Is it that other woman? The one you were engaged to?"

"No. Yes." Frustrated by the circumstances, Starbuck stood up and began to pace. "Sela's part of it," he admitted. "But not the way you think. It's just that in a very real way, she represents where I've come from. Who I am."

Sela. Now the woman—her rival—had a name, which made her much more real.

"I think you'd better tell me the whole story," she suggested with a great deal more calm than she was feeling.

Starbuck knew she was right. He owed her the truth. All of it.

He sighed. "We still have to wash that cut," he said. "Also, I should telephone Dylan and warn him that he's in possible danger. And then, I think you're right about needing something to drink."

"Is it that bad?"

"I suppose that depends on your point of view."

He returned to the bathroom long enough to re-trieve the bottle of hydrogen peroxide, some cotton balls and a towel. Dampening the cotton, he dabbed at the shallow cut.

"You're right about it only being a flesh wound," he agreed. "It's already beginning to heal."

"I told you so," she said distractedly, worried yet again about what secrets Starbuck was hiding.

Charity remembered feeling like this before. When she was six years old and the carnival had come to Cas-tle Mountain and Dylan had talked her into going to the fun house, which hadn't been any fun at all. Her nerves battering away inside her, she'd gingerly made her way through the dark and narrow hallways, waiting for some unknown monster to pop out of the shadows.

That was when she'd discovered that the monsters you can't see are more frightening than any monster you might have to face.

"There. All done." Starbuck's voice broke into her turmoiled reverie.

"You have a very gentle touch."

"Your mind was so far away I doubt if you would have felt me attacking you with a hammer and chain saw," he said mildly.

He left the room. She heard brief snatches of a con-versation she assumed was with her brother. Then he returned a moment later with two snifters of brandy.

"Dylan is concerned about you," he related. "I as-sured him that you were as well as can be expected, un-der the circumstances. I promised that I would not leave you alone."

Starbuck took a deep breath before saying, "I also informed him that I was going to tell you the truth about my mission."

"Dylan knows?"

"Everything. He cautioned me against telling you, then, when he realized I could not be dissuaded, wished me luck." He handed one of the balloon glasses to Charity. After reclaiming his spot beside her on the bed, he sat for a long silent time, swirling the liquor in his own snifter, staring down into the dark amber depths as if seeking the words to explain the unexplainable.

"I don't really know how to start," he confessed.

"Why not at the beginning?"

He laughed at that, but the sound held little humor. "The beginning," he mused. "All right."

He tossed his head back, downed the brandy in long swallows, then placed the empty glass on the table beside the bed.

"It all began," Starbuck started slowly, carefully, "in a galaxy, far, far away."

11

"I DON'T BELIEVE IT." Charity stared up at Starbuck, her eyes wide, the pain in her head forgotten during the telling of his outrageous tale.

"I can understand how it might be difficult to believe such a story," Starbuck said. "But it is true."

"You actually expect me to believe that you're an alien, come here from another planet."

"Sarnia," he agreed. "But since my mother is a terran, I suppose that only makes me a half alien. And although genetically terrans and Sarnians are nearly identical, terran physical genes usually prove dominant, so my body is human."

He didn't add that since meeting Charity, he'd also discovered a very human heart.

"You've no idea how what a relief that is," Charity said dryly.

She rubbed her arms with her hands to ward off the sudden chill caused by his calm words, his honest gaze. If she didn't know better, she'd think he was actually telling the truth.

The problem was, Charity decided, Starbuck believed he was some kind of intergalactic space traveler.

"Let's go."

When she would have left the bed, Starbuck stopped her by putting a broad hand on each shoulder. "Go? Where?"

"To the mainland."

"Why would you wish to go to the mainland?"

"We need to get you to the hospital. You obviously suffered a more serious head injury than we thought that day I found you lying on the road."

"My head is fine, Charity."

"Starbuck, listen to me." Her eyes widened, imploring him to reason. "What you're suggesting simply isn't possible."

"Not in this century," he agreed. "But it will be. At least on Sarnia."

"Sarnia." She combed a trembling hand through her hair, ruffling the strands in a way that made Starbuck long to reach out and smooth them back again. "I've never heard of a planet called Sarnia."

"I explained that," he said patiently. "It's in another galaxy."

"Far, far away. I know. And you're a member of the ruling family, descended down from the Ancient Ones who wrote a book of laws based on the ideal of truth and reason."

"That is true."

"Right. And your sister's a xenoanthropologist and you're an astrophysicist and you've been experimenting with ways to travel without a spaceship using antimatter, astro-projection and some kind of quantum physics you discovered in a book Dylan still hasn't written."

"That is also correct."

"And somehow, you managed to lock onto my thoughts and beam down, just like *Star Trek*. But the solar flares warped time, so you ended up two hundred years before you'd planned to arrive."

"Exactly." He'd known she was intelligent, but he hadn't expected her to grasp the logistics so quickly.

"That does it. We are definitely taking you to the hospital." The trick would be, Charity considered, keeping him out of the psycho wing.

"But why?"

"Because," she pointed out, "you just proved that you're hallucinating."

"I fail to comprehend your convoluted feminine reasoning."

Charity pushed down a surge of renewed anger, reminding herself that he'd obviously suffered a serious head injury and couldn't be held entirely responsible for everything he said.

"Because, if you really are from Sarnia, two hundred years in the future, how do you explain knowing about *Star Trek?*"

"Those films are classics," Starbuck argued. "Julianna has all twenty-six of the movies on holodisk in her library."

"Twenty-six? There are actually twenty-six *Star Trek* movies?"

"They were making number twenty-seven when I left Sarnia," Starbuck divulged. "The plot was carefully guarded, but there are rumors that the crew is getting a new ship. Their sixth."

"Personally, I always liked the *Enterprise,*" Charity said.

"That is my favorite, as well. And although the Sarnian Council of Arts declared the films illogical and banned their distribution on my planet more than fifty years ago, a hard-core group of fans, such as my sister, remains. So Federation traders smuggle them past customs to supply a very efficient black market."

"Twenty-six," Charity repeated softly. "Dylan would be in seventh heaven. Just last month he went to a *Star*

Trek marathon at a theater in Bangor that showed all six movies in a row. People camped out overnight for the best seats."

Realizing that she'd begun to fall into the lure of Starbuck's own crazed fantasy, she shook her head. "This is ridiculous. You almost had me believing you."

"I have not lied to you, Charity."

"Prove it."

He had never met a more stubborn woman. Except, perhaps, Starbuck considered, his sister. For all Julianna's quiet poise, she could prove frustratingly intransigent at the most inconvenient times. Such as her discomfiting search for those ancient, heretical diaries. And of course there had been that time when Zoltar Flavius, ambassador to Galactia and a man twice Julianna's age, asked their father for her hand in marriage.

At the coaxing of his terran wife, Xanthus Valderian had agreed to permit Julianna to select her own lifemate. Which proved a disastrous political mistake when the young woman refused to even consider a marriage contract with the powerful, wealthy ambassador, who, like Xanthus himself, was descended from the Ancient Ones.

News of his sister's refusal had spread throughout Sarnia, as well as the rest of the galaxy, like flashfire. Since women were not empowered to choose their own destiny, such freedom was considered abhorrent by old-line conservatives and vastly encouraging by proponents of female rights.

Unfortunately, Julianna's freedom of choice had proven to be Zoltar Flavius's public humiliation. A powerful man with a temper that was decidedly un-Sarnian, he'd effectively gotten Xanthus Valderian removed from the governing body of city states. Starbuck had suspected that his father's forced retirement had been the cause of his fatal heart attack.

Once he'd finished with her father, Xanthus had directed his fury toward Julianna. But before he could succeed in getting her fired from the institute, on the way back to Galactia, his space pod had been hit by a meteor shower, effectively putting an end to both the ambassador's life and his revenge.

"I'm waiting," Charity's voice broke into his thoughts.

"Oh. Yes." Deciding to use the same method of proof that had won Dylan over, Starbuck concentrated on sending his atoms across the room.

Something was definitely wrong. Try as he might, he couldn't generate sufficient energy.

"Oh, my God!" Charity stared at the sparkling pieces of matter, unmistakably shaped like a man, that were hovering above the very spot where Starbuck had been standing only a moment before. "I don't believe it!"

"Neither do I." Starbuck ceased trying and pulled himself together. Sweat glistened on his brow, above his upper lip. His shirt was drenched. "Even a fourth-level Sarnian should be able to project himself across such a small space. But I find it impossible. This is most disturbing."

"Is that how you reached me out in the forest without leaving footprints?"

"Yes. But at the time I did not have so much trouble." He crossed his arms and pondered that for a moment. "I don't understand."

He rubbed his square chin thoughtfully. "Perhaps it was the adrenaline," he mused. "I was aware that someone was trying to hurt you. I also knew that I had to move quickly."

"Adrenaline is supposed to give an amazing rush," Charity agreed. "I've read of cases where one-hundred-pound mothers have lifted cars off their children."

"I believe that must be the answer," Starbuck decided absently.

A terrible thought was teasing at the back of his mind. If he couldn't manage to project himself across the room, how was he ever going to return home? Even with the assistance of the accelerator and the transporter he and Dylan had finally completed last night, he needed his skills operating at top speed.

"You really are from another planet, aren't you?"

She'd written all those UFO sightings off as hysteria, caused by the solar flares. But the proof was right here, in her bedroom, only a few feet away.

"Yes. But I am not three feet tall or green complected. Nor am I dressed in Reynolds Wrap." He looked at her curiously. "What is Reynolds Wrap?"

"It's tin foil. You know, shiny and silver. We use it to wrap leftovers in."

"Ah. Tinanium sheets." Starbuck nodded. "My mother's cook does the same. But she always forgets to label them, so you can never tell what's in any of the packages."

"That happens on Earth, too."

A significant little silence settled over them.

"Starbuck?"

"Yes?"

She was looking up at him, helpless fascination mingled with longing. "I can see that you're not green, or silver, and you don't have a face like a vacuum cleaner hose, but you said you were only half Sarnian, and your body, like your mother's, is completely human. Does that mean..."

Color flooded her face as her voice tailed off. "Never mind." Suffused with embarrassment, she turned away.

He didn't need to read her mind to know what she was thinking. The feminine invitation had been gleaming in her soft blue eyes.

Slowly, deliberately, Starbuck crossed the room on foot and reclaimed his place on the edge of the bed. "Are you asking if I make love like the men you're accustomed to sleeping with?"

"Yes." She looked up at him, silent, questioning, wanting him more than she'd ever wanted any man in her life.

"I don't know what kind of man you're accustomed to," he reminded her. "So, I suppose there's only one way to find out."

Her lips curved into a soft smile. "I was rather hoping that you'd come to that conclusion."

He was being unfair to her. He wanted her, with every fiber of his being. And even more remarkable was the knowledge that he loved Charity Prescott even more than he wanted her.

But he couldn't stay. And he sure as hell couldn't take her with him. So where did that leave them?

Nowhere, Starbuck acknowledged grimly. Nowhere at all.

"Charity." His voice was a rasp of agony. "I don't want to lie to you, sweetheart. This can't go anywhere."

She was trembling with a need like nothing she'd ever known. Every pore on her body was aching for this man's touch.

"Too late," she answered on a short, shaky laugh that was every bit as unsteady as her pulse. "It already has."

Wrapping her arms around his neck, she pulled him down to her and pressed her mouth against his. Hard.

He wanted to take things slowly. Carefully. And not just for her, Starbuck realized. But for himself. He wanted to savor the moment, to create a memory that would unite them through the years and miles and miles of space that would soon separate them.

Her lips were soft and trembling, but avid and mobile beneath his. And so, so sweet.

Scents. Remarkably, love had scents. They rose from her warming flesh, surrounding him in a dense, fragrant cloud. He breathed in the intoxicating scent of her hair and knew that he'd never see flowers again without thinking of this woman.

Tastes. Amazingly, love had tastes. The honey taste of her lips, the sweet, moist, sunshine taste of her warming flesh. These and countless other seductive flavors lingered on his tongue, spun in his head.

Feelings bombarded him. Emotions too numerous to catalogue rushed over him, until he felt as if he were drowning in them.

"I've been dreaming of this," she whispered as she slipped her hands beneath his sweater and ran her hands over his back. "I've been dreaming of you." She pressed her lips against his neck. "Wicked, wanton, wonderful dreams."

Her breathless admission excited him. Tangling his hands in her hair, he kissed her hard and long. Needs poured out of him and into her. Love flowed out of her and into him.

Beneath him, Charity's body was soft and pliant, but he could feel the strength there, as well. Charity Prescott was forged steel wrapped in shimmering folds of silk. Starbuck found the combination impossible to resist.

For fifteen of his thirty years, Starbuck had always regarded the taking off of one's clothes as little more than a prelude to sex. But now, as he pulled her blue uniform shirt loose and began to unbutton it, one button at a time, he realized that undressing Charity was every bit as sensuous an experience as the heady taste of her kisses.

With fingers he wished were steadier, he maneuvered each button through the hole, then folded back the material slowly, tenderly. He smiled when he saw she was wearing the peach confection she'd worn in her erotic dream.

"You can't tell me this is regulation for members of the Castle Mountain police force." As he'd done in the dream, he ran his finger over the lace trimming the bodice.

"No." Charity sucked in a deep breath as the light touch left a shimmering trail of heat. "It's not."

"Good." He lowered his head and pressed his open mouth against her breast, dampening the silk in a slow, sensual way that caused a corresponding dampness between her legs.

"I like knowing that there's a sexy, feminine part of you that you keep hidden away." When his teeth closed, taking a nip of silk and nipple, Charity moaned and moved against him. "I like being the man to discover your private secrets."

The fire was building. Utilizing every atom of his hard-learned self-control, Starbuck banked it. For now.

He released the buttons on the cuffs of her shirt. Her body arched as he drew it away. And then his hands moved to her belt. A man's belt, Starbuck thought, smiling at her thinking she could conceal so much vibrant femininity with these masculine trappings.

The belt gone, he unfastened the wool pants and drew them slowly over her stomach, her hips, down her legs, inch by maddening inch, following the path with his mouth.

Her wool socks followed, and, lifting her legs one at a time, Starbuck placed a sizzling kiss against the arch of each slender foot.

He whisked the peach silk away.

"I knew it," he murmured against her mouth as his hands fondled her breasts.

"Knew what?" she gasped.

"That your skin would be even softer than that silk."

And then his mouth was everywhere, creating heat and flames wherever it lingered. On her breasts, her thighs, the back of her knee, the beauty mark at the base of her spine, her shoulders. And even as she waited for Starbuck to take, he continued to give.

She had dreamed of this. For years. But never, in all her fantasies could she have imagined such raw hunger. Such burning need.

The heat was unbearable. She writhed on the flowered sheets; her body became slick with sweat. She begged Starbuck over and over again, in word and in desperate action, to end this torment, but still he continued, driving her higher with only his mouth and his clever, wicked hands.

Dreams became reality, wishes were fulfilled.

Her own hands clawed at the sheets; she tossed her head back and forth, her hair resembling a shimmering copper fan against the flowered pillowcase. She wanted to cry out his name, but the only sound that escaped from between her parted lips was a whisper.

"Starbuck."

His teeth nipped the delicate skin at the inside of her thighs, but there was no pain. Only more need.

"Not yet." His tongue soothed the flesh his teeth had marked. "I want you to remember this." His breath was a hot sirocco, blowing through the triangular nest of soft flame hair that concealed her most feminine secrets. "I want you to remember me."

"How could I ever forget?" she gasped as his mouth moved to that nub of exquisitely sensitive flesh.

She arched against him, bowstring taut, offering, begging, challenging as with only his mouth, he took her to the very edge of reason. Then beyond.

Shards of light and heat arced from that sensitive core, shooting outward throughout her body in a surge of shimmering golden release.

He held her, waiting for her trembling to cease. And when it finally did, he stood up and stripped off his jeans, briefs and sweater.

Charity gazed up at him, taking in the breadth of his wide shoulders, the muscular torso covered by a dark arrowing of hair, his strong dark legs, and realized that while he might be half Sarnian, he certainly looked all human male. And a very aroused one at that.

"Do you know how long I've waited for this?" he asked as he returned to the bed and drew her against him. "How long I've been waiting to lie with you like this?"

"All of two and a half weeks?"

He heard the faint edge of regret creep into her tone and did his best to kiss it away. "All my life," he corrected after they'd come up for air.

His dark fingers curved around her waist, pulling her on top of him. When she felt his hard shaft probing at the entrance to her body, Charity momentarily stiffened.

"It's okay," he soothed, putting his hand between them, stroking her tender flesh. "You're so warm. And wet. And so very, very tight."

He slid one finger into her moist heat, then another, tenderly preparing her body to accept his. "I promise we'll take it very, very slowly, Charity. I'd never hurt you."

His stroking touch was creating a renewed desire. Suddenly, without warning, Charity was caught up in another hot, sensual storm. Her body clutched desperately at his fingers, needing more.

He withdrew his hand, and as they watched each other, Charity drew him into her soft sheath. He was huge, and if she'd tensed even the slightest bit, she never would have been able to manage it, but the honest tenderness in his gaze encouraged her to relax and soon he was deep inside her, stretching her, becoming a part of her.

Charity splayed her fingers against his chest, and she met his smoky gaze as she began to move slowly, gliding up and down, loving the feel of him inside her. Loving him.

Excitement began to rise, even higher and hotter than before. She tilted her head back, closed her eyes and pressed her knees against his hips as she began to move in a rhythm as old as the forces that had formed both their universes.

Starbuck realized, with a sudden blinding clarity that he would never find another woman so perfectly matched to him as this one was. He could search all the galaxies through several lifetimes and never meet another woman so perfectly tuned, both mentally and physically, to him.

To Starbuck, making love to Charity was like being given a forbidden glimpse into a secret world. The idea of spending the rest of his days without her was impossible. But what choice did he have?

Before he could come up with a logical solution, logic disintegrated, reason dissolved and there was only now. Only this mind-shattering feeling of absolute, amazing abandon.

Experiencing the first physical orgasm of his life, Starbuck's first thought was that he was dying. The second and more powerful thought was that he had found the mythical heaven so many terrans seemed to believe in.

His last coherent thought was that he never would have imagined it possible to experience triumph and defeat at the same time.

CHARITY LAY steeped in sensation, the blood pounding in her veins, her limbs as limp as wet spaghetti, as a series of aftershocks quaked through her body.

"I never knew," she whispered. Awe and a newfound womanly awareness darkened her eyes and made her voice husky.

"I know."

She feigned a pout at his blatant masculine pride. "Once again I'm fascinated at how the male ego manages to transcend normal realms of time and space."

"This has nothing to do with ego," Starbuck argued. "Male or otherwise." He ran his palm up the back of her leg, over her rounded buttocks to rest at the base of her spine. "I knew what you were thinking, my love, because I happened to be thinking exactly the same thing."

"Oh." She rather liked the idea that what they'd just shared was as important to him as it had been to her.

"I experienced my first sexual encounter on my name day," Starbuck explained, "when I turned fifteen. But lovemaking on Sarnia is not the same as it is here on Earth."

She had to ask. "Is it better?"

She could feel his deep, rich chuckle against her breasts. "I always considered it quite satisfying," he allowed. "For a purely mental experience. I have recently discovered that there is much to be said for human physicality."

"You've never made physical love before?"

"No."

"Then how did you . . ."

She looked away, unreasonably embarrassed at the question, which was ridiculous, Charity told herself, since she and Starbuck had been about as intimate as two people could be.

"Know what to do?"

"Yes."

He ran his hand lazily down her body, from her shoulder to her thigh. "I simply followed my instincts."

"Your instincts are very good." Better than good. They were mind shattering.

"Ah, but you provided all the inspiration."

His deep voice, rough with emotion, curled around her like a warm woolen blanket. She looked up at him, her heart in her eyes.

"I love you, Starbuck."

"And I love you, Charity Prescott." He looked down at her, his gaze as sober as she'd ever seen it. "With my entire human body. And every atom of my Sarnian mind."

She heard the regret in his voice, read it in his eyes. "But it doesn't change anything, does it? Not really."

"No."

He'd tried to warn her. Tried to warn himself. But the chemistry between them, the emotional bond, had been too strong from the beginning.

He framed her sweet, heartbreakingly sad face with his hands. "I wish I could say it did. But it doesn't."

Then he took her hand and lifted it to his lips, his eyes on hers as he kissed her fingers, one at a time. "I have to return home, Charity. I have my work, my family, my life—"

"I know." She pressed her free hand against his lips, unwilling to listen to any more logical reasons why they could not spend the rest of their lives together. In Castle Mountain. In her house and in her bed.

"Don't talk," she said desperately, pulling him onto her, drawing him into her again. "Not now. For now, I just want you to make love to me again."

Having once tasted the forbidden fruit of sexual pleasures, Starbuck was ravenous. His own desires no less fevered than Charity's, he willingly complied.

Again and again, all night long.

12

WHEN THEY DIDN'T make love, they talked. Charity wanted to know everything about Sarnia, and Starbuck tried, as best he could, to explain his home planet, skimming over the part about it being a tightly held patriarchal society. He was feeling too good to get into yet another argument concerning female equality. Besides, his time with Charity had made him realize that his sister's arguments had some merit.

"What about Earth in your time?" Charity asked. She sat up in bed, pulled her knees to her chest and wrapped her arms around them.

"It's still spinning," Starbuck said.

"That's good news in itself," she decided. "That we haven't managed to blow it up or pollute it out of existence. What about California? Has it dropped into the sea yet?"

"No. But a major earthquake is due any time."

She laughed at that. "It's nice to know some things stay the same.... What about the homeless? And the forests?"

"A coalition of government and private enterprise solved the homeless problem in the twenty-first century," Starbuck told her. "The forests, unfortunately, have gone. Although third- and fourth-growth forests were farmed, eventually the harvesting became too expensive and wood products were replaced by superior amalgams."

"Oh, I hate that idea." She sighed and shook her head. "Well, we'll just have to change the future," she decided. "Have we had a woman president yet?"

"Five."

"Well, that's good news. What about the New York Yankees? Are they still on a losing streak?"

"I'm afraid so."

Another sigh. "Damn."

"But they have a new owner, so fans are hopeful," Starbuck tacked on, in hopes of putting a smile on her face. His strategy worked.

"This is so amazing." She shook her head and looked at him, her eyes moving slowly over his face, as if memorizing his features. "I never, in a million years, would have imagined that I'd be lying in bed with a Sarnian astrophysicist."

Something occurred to her. "Your name. Is it really yours?" She hated thinking that she might have cried out a false name during their lovemaking.

"It's mine," Starbuck assured her. "My birth name was Bram Valderian. Valderian is my family name. But when males reach the age of maturity, they are encouraged to choose a name they feel explains their philosophy of life."

"So you chose Starbuck because you're an astrophysicist and study stars?"

"Partly. But I mainly selected it because of several books belonging to my mother I had read as a youth."

"What books?"

"*Treasure Island* and *Captain Blood*. And, in some way, *Peter Pan*. I enjoyed reading about the exploits of Earth's pirates—they reminded me of the space buccaneers that roam our galaxy."

"Those novels were romanticized ideals," she felt obliged to point out.

"True. But, against logic, something about the lives of those corsairs appealed to me."

"Perhaps it was exactly because they were against logic. They were rebels in a carefully stratified society. Perhaps choosing Starbuck for your name was your way of expressing your own inner feelings of frustration."

He ran his hand down her hair and drew her close. "How do you know me so well?" he murmured against the top of her head.

She looked up at him and smiled. "Simple. I love you. And," she reminded him, "I seem to be able to read your mind."

"Can you tell what I'm thinking now?"

She took a long time, pretending to look deep into his steady gaze. "You want to make love to me."

"That's very good."

"It was also easy," she said on a soft laugh. She ran her hand over the sheet that was tented over his lower torso. "Since your Sarnian mind keeps sending the same message to your very human body."

Laughing, she pulled the sheet away and drew him to her. That was all either of them was to say for a very long time.

PINK FINGERS OF DAWN were spreading across a pearl-gray sky. Unbelievably, almost twenty-four hours had passed. Starbuck and Charity were sitting at the kitchen table, watching a family of deer at the salt lick behind her house.

"The paper says that syzygy occurs this evening," Charity murmured.

Sometime, during the long, love-filled night, Starbuck had told her of Dylan's belief that the upcoming arrangement of planets—lined up along the same radius and along the same orbital plane extending from the sun—could provide the optimum time for Starbuck's departure.

Charity realized with a certain detached wonder that the idea of Starbuck leaving her was more shattering than the fact that she'd managed to fall in love with a man not only from another planet but another time, as well.

"Yes." Starbuck couldn't look at her. His heart was already aching at the idea of leaving.

"So, we only have today."

"Not even that." He felt her intense disappointment. "I have to spend the day in the lab."

"But I thought you and Dylan had come up with the coordinates."

"We have. But now I have to come up with some way to boost my projection power. It's obvious that something about Earth's atmosphere or gravity is blocking my abilities. Ever since my arrival, I've been mind-blind—"

"Not with me," Charity pointed out.

"No." Starbuck smiled, took her hand and linked their fingers together atop the maple table. "Not with you. But without a ship, my entire theory depends on my being able to achieve absolute astro-projection. As you saw earlier, I can no longer achieve the proper level."

"Does that mean you're going to have to call off the experiment?" That you'll be forced to stay here? With me? she wondered but didn't dare ask.

"It does unless I can get my hands on some diamaziman crystals within the next six hours," he agreed.

"Diamaziman?"

"A carbon-based stone, whose atoms have been crystallized into a solid cubic pattern," he explained. "Blue diamaziman is preferable, because it possesses the impurity boron, which serves as an electrical conductor. On Sarnia, such diamaziman is utilized to beam down visitors who do not possess the ability of astro-projection."

Starbuck remembered how many times he'd considered those individuals without such ability inferior, and he felt humbled. And ashamed.

"There's nothing else you could use?"

"No." He frowned and dragged his hand through his hair. "It is, of course, possible to create diamaziman in a laboratory setting, by placing graphite, which is pure carbon, along with a metal solvent between tungsten-carbide pistons and subjecting them to a pressure of a million pounds per square inch, then heating them to thirty-five hundred of your Fahrenheit degrees.

"But your technology is behind ours. It would take at least a week to produce a usable diamaziman."

"And you don't have a week."

"No." Starbuck heard the regret in her voice, felt it in his own heart. "I don't."

It was Charity's turn to sigh.

A silence descended. Outside the kitchen window, the birds had gathered for their morning meal. The cat sat on the windowsill, growling and batting impotently at the feathered visitors through the double-pane glass. Lost in her turmoiled thoughts, Charity ignored both birds and cat.

"Wait here," she said finally. She rose from the table and left the room. When she returned, she was carrying a small gray box, which she held out to Starbuck.

"Maybe this will help," she suggested in a quiet voice.

He took the box and lifted the lid. Inside, resting on a bed of pearl-gray velvet, was a perfect marquise-cut blue diamaziman set in a platinum band.

Startled, Starbuck looked up at her.

"It was my engagement ring," she answered his unspoken question. "After my marriage disintegrated, I didn't want it. I walked along the beach, determined to toss the damn thing into the surf. But, being Yankee born and bred, I couldn't bear to toss away a valuable diamond, so I kept it."

"You could have sold it," Starbuck suggested. He ran his finger over the dazzling blue stone. "I imagine it is quite valuable."

"Probably." Charity shrugged. "I considered that idea and rejected it." A soft, thoughtful look came into her eyes. "Perhaps, intuitively, I knew that someday I'd have a much better use for it."

He glanced around her homey, comfortably shabby kitchen, thinking that she could undoubtedly use the funds such a stone would bring.

"I appreciate your generous gesture, Charity," Starbuck said, giving the stone one last look before closing the box with a snap, "but I cannot take such a valuable gift."

"It's only money," she argued. What she didn't say was that she'd given him something far more valuable. Her heart.

"Tell me about him," Starbuck said suddenly. "Tell me about the man who gave you this ring." Even in his own time, such a stone would be worth a virtual fortune. Starbuck tried to envision Charity as a wife of such a wealthy man and failed.

Charity shrugged. "He was an actor. A star, actually," she said. "On television. Movies." Something occurred to her. "His name is Steven Stone."

Starbuck knew exactly why she'd asked. "The name means nothing."

"Good." She nodded. "I'd hate to find out that such a lying rat had been able to maintain his popularity for centuries."

"I can't imagine you as the wife of a movie actor," Starbuck ventured.

"Neither could Steven. We met when I was assigned to a security detail when he did a public appearance at a mall in Venice. He told me I was the most beautiful woman in the world."

"I thought you said he was a liar."

She shot him a quick, appreciative smile. "Flatterer."

"I find you the most beautiful woman in all the worlds I've ever traveled."

The compliment, like so many of Starbuck's statements was simply, honestly spoken. It also went directly to her heart.

"Well." Charity took a deep breath. "Anyway, the next thing I knew, I received an offer to act as a technical adviser on his series. I suppose I was flattered by his constant, unrelenting attention, or stardust got into my eyes, or I just liked the idea of seeing my name on the television screen every Wednesday night.

"Whatever, I finally agreed. At the end of that season, we were married." A soft shadow moved across her eyes. "Six months later, my father had his heart attack. I came home to Maine for the funeral. I returned to Malibu to find that week's romantic costar playing a starring role in my bed."

She shook her head with self-disgust. "Later I discovered that Steven had a reputation for bedding them all. The rest of the crew referred to the actresses as the girl of the week." Her laugh was short and bitter. Like her marriage, Charity considered.

"I was angry, hurt and humiliated. So I returned to Castle Mountain to lick my wounds. That's when I discovered I belonged here. So I stayed.... Now tell me about Sela."

"She is a perfect Sarnian," Starbuck said. "Calm, utterly logical and unerringly precise. She is a time-management consultant."

"She sounds boring," Charity decided.

Starbuck laughed at that. "She is. But we were matched at a very early age by our parents, so, until I disgraced her with my dismissal from the space council, neither of us ever questioned such arrangement."

Charity knew that his alleged disgrace would immediately turn to triumph when he returned to Sarnia. Undoubtedly the utterly logical Sela would be quick to change her mind about calling off their marriage.

"And now?" She had to ask.

"And now I know that I could never bond with her. Because my heart, and all my thoughts will belong to you."

He looked down at the ring for a long, thoughtful time, then up at Charity. "You realize, that without this diamaziman, I probably could not return to Sarnia."

"Yes." Her lips were unbearably dry. She had to push the single softly spoken word past the lump in her throat.

"Then why?"

Tears stung at the back of her lids, and Charity resolutely blinked them away. "I understand your need to return to your own world, your own time," she said. "And if there's any way I can help, I will."

What she didn't tell him was that the thought of his molecules scattered all over space because he'd lacked the power to complete his projection was too horrifying to contemplate.

Starbuck studied her for a long, thoughtful moment. Conflicting emotions raged inside him.

Go. Stay. Duty. Love. Family. Charity.

Logic warred with sentiment, his head waged battle with his newly discovered heart.

He wanted to promise that he would come back, but he didn't. His life was on Sarnia.

She smiled, but her lips trembled and the hot tears that had been threatening made her eyes glisten in a way that Starbuck found more painful than any physical wound could ever be.

A single tear trailed down her cheek. When Starbuck tenderly brushed it away with his thumb, she had to choke back a sob.

"I don't want to talk anymore," she said in a frail, fractured voice. She looked up at him, all the love she felt for this man shining on her face, gleaming in her eyes. "Make love to me, Starbuck." She did not care how needy such a plea might sound; at this moment, she would have begged.

Starbuck needed no second invitation.

Hand in hand, they walked into the bedroom. And although she never would have thought it possible, this time the passion burned even higher between them and the hunger was even more intense.

And then, as if by mutual unspoken consent, they slowed the pace. It was as if they both knew that this was the last time they would be together this way and both wanted to create a memory that would last throughout the ages that would soon separate them.

There were no whispered words of love, no wild, rash promises. They spoke with soft sighs and inarticulate murmurs. They spoke with touches, the brush of a fingertip along the curve of a lip, the press of a palm against warming flesh.

A wintry sun crept above the horizon, creating a misty glow and dappling their skin with frail, stuttering light. Charity felt his hands slide over her, felt his breath warming her flesh.

"Would you do something for me?" she whispered.

His lips plucked at hers. "Anything."

It was not quite the truth and they both knew it.

"Make love to me the way you would on Sarnia."

Startled, Starbuck braced himself up on one elbow. "You wouldn't like it."

"How do you know? If you don't try?"

"It's not nearly as fulfilling as the Earthly way," Starbuck argued. His body was aching to sheathe itself once again in her silken warmth; the purely mental sexual encounter he'd always found satisfying paled in comparison.

"Please?" She ran her fingernail down his chest and gave him a melting, sensual smile. "Just this once?"

He could, Starbuck considered, deny this woman nothing. He was grateful that she was too honorable to ask him to stay in Castle Mountain, Maine. Because if she ever made such a request and looked up at him with those incredible blue eyes, Starbuck knew he'd never see Sarnia again.

"All right. But don't say I didn't warn you." He gave her one last, long, deep kiss to satisfy himself, then said, "We have to kneel facing one another."

"On the bed? Or would the floor be better?"

Starbuck sighed. Sweet Valhalla, how he hated the idea of leaving the warm, love-rumpled sheets. "I suppose the floor would be a superior surface," he agreed.

"How do you do it on Sarnia?"

"On a thin pallet on the floor."

"Well, then, the rug should work." She left the bed and knelt on the rag rug in front of the fire.

Grumbling, Starbuck joined her. The sensual mood, unsurprisingly, was gone, chased away with the need to explain the logistics of Sarnian sex.

He knelt in front of her. "Now we touch palms."

"Like this?" She pressed her hands against his.

"Exactly. You must remember, this will be purely mental, a melding of thoughts."

"I can't wait."

It was obviously true, Starbuck realized with surprise. She was so excited she was trembling.

Starbuck thought the experience would be typically passionless. He was wrong.

With only their fingertips touching, they tenderly explored each other's consciousness, their entwined thoughts exploring realms of sensuality beyond anything either of them had known.

The room became bathed in a warm, flickering glow. Swirling lights—royal blue, blazing scarlet, gleaming gold and shimmering silver—surrounded them.

Incredibly, there was music, the hot, poignant sound of alto sax bringing to mind steamy nights and sensual summer days.

Three-dimensional images of themselves making
love in myriad ways and places appeared. Together
they watched themselves sitting in a meadow, surrounded by wildflowers.

Charity was wearing a gossamer white dress made
of some type of gauze, he was clad in a flowing white
poet's shirt and black pants reminiscent of a pirate's.
Starbuck was weaving a coronet of sunshine-yellow
flowers, which he placed atop her coppery head.

Then, slowly, they undressed each other, and as he
laid her back among the flowers and slipped into her,
the vision shifted, like the facets of a kaleidoscope, and
they were lying on the deck of a tall-masted ship that
was plowing through the waves.

They were in the midst of a squall, but caught up in
their own passion, neither noticed the bucking of the
schooner, the pelting rain, the moaning wind. Starbuck was draping a king's ransom in ice-blue dia-
monds over her nude body, while telling her how
beautiful, how desirable she was and all the wild, erotic
things he was going to do to her, and Charity was saying yes, yes, to everything.

And then they were lying on some golden beach, beside a blue lagoon while gentle trade winds made the
palm trees sway overhead. And they were making
love—wonderful, glorious love—as the warm water
lapped against the golden sand and the sun shone be-
nevolently overhead, and when they climaxed together, their spirits soared away from their bodies on
gossamer wings, flying directly into the bright and
glowing sun.

And then they were back in her bedroom and Starbuck realized that tears were flowing down his face.

He'd never felt anything like it, he'd never known that it was possible to experience such pure sweet pleasure.

Together they lowered their hands, but not yet ready to draw apart, they linked their fingers together and remained, bonded, mind and body and soul.

"I thought you'd taught me true passion earlier." Her voice was only a whisper, but easily heard in the stillness of the room. "But I'd never, in a million years, imagined..."

"I know." He drew her close and pressed his wet cheek against hers. "I, too, had not known such pleasure was possible."

The strength of the emotions they'd shared left them both exhausted. Arms wrapped around each other, they lay down on the rug and surrendered to a deep, blissful sleep.

ALL TOO SOON, reality returned.

Starbuck stood in the kitchen doorway, frustration etched onto his handsome face.

He'd invited Charity—coming perilously close to begging—to return to the lab with him, to see him off. But she'd refused, saying that she wanted to remember him here, in her house, where they'd shared so much love.

"I hate leaving you."

"I know." Charity was out of tears. All she had left was a terrible empty hole where her heart used to be. "But it's important that you return to Sarnia and prove you were right."

He ran the back of his hand down her too-pale face. "If I could, I'd take you with me."

"I know. But the diamond will only provide enough strength for one." She gave him her bravest smile, but it wobbled dangerously, then collapsed completely.

"I'm sorry." Turning away, Charity buried her face in her hands and took several deep, calming breaths.

When she turned back to him, her expression was composed, although renewed tears shone wetly in her eyes. "Have a safe journey, Starbuck."

For some reason he could not discern, her stalwart bravery, at a time when he knew her heart was breaking, made him want to cry.

"I will never forget you."

She took his hand in hers and pressed it against her heart. "Nor I you. Across time I will love you."

"And across space I will love you."

They could have been speaking their marriage vows, Starbuck considered. Their minds tangled and he knew that Charity was thinking the same thing.

Because the one thing that neither time nor distance could ever alter was that they belonged together. And they both knew that they would never forsake each other.

"I remember reading something, once," Charity said. "If two hearts are truly bonded, if two people are meant to be together, they will find each other. No matter what obstacles come between them."

Her hand tightened and her eyes grew moist again. "We are bonded, Starbuck. Hearts and minds and souls.

"And the only reason I can send you away, back to your home, is that I know, with every fiber of my being, that we will find each other again."

Logic told him that she was being an overly romantic female.

His heart told Starbuck that she spoke the truth.

"We will be together," he agreed. "Someday. For always."

She bit her lip and refused to cry. Outside the open door, the waiting birds became more vocal, demanding their breakfast.

"For always," she whispered.

He drew her to him and they came together, body to body, mouth to mouth. His heartbeat was quick and hard against her as he succumbed to her softness, her strength. Her hands tangled in his hair as she submerged herself to his will, his tenderness.

And with one last reluctant, regretful touch of his hand to her hair, he was walking toward the shiny black snowmobile Dylan had lent him.

Charity stood at the window and watched Starbuck drive away. Back to his own life. His own time.

13

DESPERATELY TRYING to keep her mind off what Starbuck and Dylan were doing at the brain factory, Charity spent the morning cleaning out her desk.

She hadn't had the heart to do it before. Too many things that reminded her of her father, and how much she missed him, were buried in the bits of papers and various small treasures her father, an incorrigible pack rat, had saved.

She found memos he'd written to himself—domestic little notes reminding him to bring home milk or bread after work, forgotten immediately after having been written. There was a newspaper clipping from the *Castle Mountain Yankee Observer*, detailing how a hometown girl, Charity Prescott, had been assigned to be a technical adviser on a television series in Hollywood. The article, written by Mildred Cummings, the *Observer*'s long-time social editor, gushed effusively, making Charity sound like a movie star herself.

There were other clippings regarding her work—specifically her apprehension of the Surfer rapist, and an equal number relating Dylan's various awards and achievements.

There were birthday cards, sketched by her artist mother. After reading the suggestive, highly personal message her mother had written inside the first card, Charity resisted opening the others. And although it did not come as a surprise to discover that her parents had remained very much in love both physically and emotionally during their thirty-five years of marriage, Charity found herself experiencing a definite twinge of envy.

"Damn." She jabbed her finger on one of the trout flies her father was all the time tying. When a tiny spot of blood appeared on the tip of her finger, she stuck it in her mouth.

And that's when she saw it. A vision appeared in her mind, a three-dimensional image so real that she felt she could reach out and touch it.

Starbuck was in danger. As was Dylan. They were in the lab, the barrel of a gun pointed directly at them. As hard as Charity tried, she couldn't see who was holding the gun.

After calling Andy on the radio, telling him to meet her at the lab, she ran out to the Jeep and drove, hell-bent for leather, to the wooded site. Although the temperature was in the low thirties, Charity's hands were slick with sweat as they gripped the steering wheel.

She said Starbuck's name over and over again, like a talisman. Like a prayer.

The odometer on the dash clicked away the tenths of miles; unfortunately, the clock beside it was also ticking away precious minutes.

All the time, she tried to focus on the image, but it had faded away, like morning fog over the harbor. Fear coalesced into a tight cold ball in her throat as she was forced to wonder if the reason she could no longer read Starbuck's mind was because he was no longer alive.

She stopped the Jeep in the trees, not wanting to pull up into the clearing right in front of the lab. She wished there was some way to sneak into the building; unfortunately, Dylan had installed a state-of-the-art security system. The slightest attempt to break in would set off a series of computerized alarms.

"Hello. May I have your name, please," the computerized female voice requested as Charity stopped in front of the door.

"Charity Prescott," Charity obliged, hoping the bite of frustration in her tone would not screw up the voiceprint.

It didn't. "Thank you, Charity Prescott," the disembodied voice continued. "Now may I request a handprint, please."

Every nerve end in her body was screaming as she wondered what, exactly, was happening inside the building. But she placed her hand against the screen as instructed.

"Working," the voice assured her. "Scan completed. You may enter, Charity Prescott."

"It's about time," Charity muttered as the door obligingly slid open.

"Have a nice day," the voice responded.

So far, so good. She was in the building. Now all she had to do was find Starbuck and Dylan and get them both out of here without anyone getting killed.

The building was strangely deserted. At first that puzzled Charity, then she realized that Dylan must have sent everyone else home in order to keep Starbuck's departure a secret.

Even as she tried her best to tread carefully, the heels of her boots seemed to echo noisily on the tile floor. As she headed down the hallway toward Dylan's lab, Charity wished that she possessed Starbuck's ability for astro-projection.

AT THE MOMENT, Starbuck wasn't projecting anywhere. In fact, he felt as if his boots were nailed to the floor.

Having never been accustomed to violence on his own planet, Starbuck found this entire scenario extremely distasteful. And illogical.

"I do not understand how you believe you are going to get away with this," he said, biting back his anger, instinctively knowing that giving in to his seething rage would only make matters worse.

"It's actually quite simple," Vanessa responded with a cold smile that matched the glittery frost in her eyes. "While I hold this lethal weapon on the two of you, Brian and Murph—" she gestured toward the two men standing on either side of her, looking like muscle-bound linemen flanking their quarterback "—will gather up all the data disks for the Way-Back machine our boy genius here has created and take them out of here. Next they'll escort you out to the secured van we have waiting.

"Then, unfortunately, some unstable substance is going to leak out of the chem lab down the hall and explode into a gigantic fireball that will level the laboratory.

"By the time they manage to dig whatever remains of Dylan's body from the rubble, I will be in Paris, sipping champagne on the Champs-Élysées."

"Who are you working for?" Dylan asked, genuinely curious. "CIA? Some crazy terrorist group?"

She laughed at that, but the harsh sound held no humor. "I told my father that you'd never make the connection."

Dylan's blue eyes narrowed. "You're Harlan Klinghofer's daughter." It was not a question.

"Bull's-eye. Give the man a Kewpie doll."

"I should have realized," Dylan muttered, shaking his head in self-disgust. "I should have seen the resemblance."

"But I don't look anything like my father."

"Yes, you do," Dylan corrected. "You both have the same glitter of avarice in your eyes." He cursed. "I should have figured it out."

"Oh, I wouldn't be so hard on yourself, darling," Vanessa advised. "After all, you were rather wrapped up in your work. Not to mention your little alien friend here."

Her eyes glittered with that very avarice Dylan had accused her of possessing as she glanced over at Starbuck, who had been watching the exchange with interest. "In case you hadn't realized it," she said, "you are worth your weight in gold."

"Why are you doing this?" Starbuck asked. A whitehot rage was building inside him at the realization that this was the person responsible for injuring Charity. With a mighty effort, Starbuck forced it down. For now.

"Why, to advance the cause of science, of course," she said.

"Not to mention the dough involved," Dylan added. "Especially since your father lost his government funding."

"Because you stole his work," Vanessa snapped.

"The quantum jump time travel and antimatter work was always mine," Dylan argued. "I created it, I nurtured it, I'm the one that did all the work. But your father was too greedy and too impatient, so he couldn't resist stealing the concept from one of his own men, twisting the data to make it look as if we were further along than we were, then offering it to the highest bidder."

"God, you are naive. That's the way the game is played," she ground out. "It all would have worked out. All of us could have been rich, Dylan, but you had to blow the whistle."

"I wasn't going to let the Pentagon get their grubby little hands on my work and turn it into the latest high-tech war machine."

"Well, now you don't have any choice, do you?" Gesturing toward the computer with the revolver, she said to the enormous man she'd called Murph, "Tie these two up to keep them out of trouble, then start loading this stuff, along with Mr. Spock, into the van. We've wasted enough time as it is."

Starbuck exchanged a glance with Dylan, who nodded imperceptibly. A moment later, all hell broke loose.

"What the—"

One of Vanessa's goons, the one who'd been about to tie the rope around Starbuck's wrists, gaped at the spot his quarry had been standing. A second later, a hand pressed against the back of his head, and he crumpled to the floor.

At the same time, Dylan lowered his head and rammed it into the stomach of the walking Coke machine headed his way. He was rewarded by a heavy *oof,* as the man's air was forced from his lungs. A moment later, Dylan felt a bullet whiz past his ear and he dived for the floor.

"Damn it, Vanessa," he ground out as he rolled under a desk, "aren't you carrying this quest for knowledge a little bit too far?"

The only answer was a bullet splintering the wood only inches from his head.

Dylan cursed when he saw Murph was back on his feet and headed his way. He tipped the desk over, scattering papers. With an angry roar, the man kicked the desk aside, shattering it as if it had been made of balsa wood.

But Dylan had already moved on.

"You're not going to get away," Vanessa warned.

"I believe that's my line," Charity said calmly, her own weapon aimed point-blank at the woman she'd never liked. "At the risk of sounding clichéd, drop the gun, Vanessa."

Vanessa wasn't about to throw in the towel yet. "Murph, get the alien."

"That's what I'm trying to do, damn it," he complained, furious that every time he neared Starbuck, the man would dematerialize, then pop up somewhere else across the room. Finally, frustrated, he charged.

Dylan, crouched behind a bookcase, stuck out his leg. As he watched the giant go tumbling to the floor, he called out cheerfully, "Timber."

Vanessa, faced with the inevitable, let loose with a string of curses that would have made a Maine lumberjack blush. Then, furious, she obediently dropped her weapon to the floor.

Breathing again, Charity whipped out her handcuffs and snapped them around the woman's wrists.

Two minutes later, Andy arrived with the police van to pick up the unholy trio. As Charity handed the prisoners over to her deputy, she gave in to temptation and issued an order she'd been dying to say for years.

"Book 'em, Andy."

SHE SHOULD BE FLYING. After all, it wasn't every day the police chief of a quiet little town like Castle Mountain had the opportunity to save her brother and lover from a potential murderer, not to mention the little fact that she'd kept a major scientific breakthrough from somehow being turned into yet another doomsday machine by war profiteers.

But she couldn't be happy. Because the one thing that hadn't changed was that Starbuck was leaving.

They were standing alone in the lab, hands linked, minds entwined.

"I thought you'd lost your powers," she said, seeking something, anything to say.

"I have, for the most part," he agreed. "But I believe you're right about the adrenaline rush. There's something very primitive about fighting for your life." But it had been more than that, he knew. Revenge had driven him. Revenge for Vanessa having harmed the woman he loved.

"I don't imagine you have much opportunity to do that on Sarnia."

He almost smiled at that. "No. So long as you stay out of the taverns frequented by outlanders, Sarnia is unrelentingly peaceful."

"Violence is illogical," she agreed softly.

"That's the downside," he said. "But during my time on Earth, I have come to realize that absolute logic is not the utopia it is made out to be." He drew her close and pressed his lips against her hair. "Because of you, I have discovered that the very best things in life are sometimes the most illogical."

She smiled up at him through misty eyes. "Ah, we're back to me being an illogical female again?"

He traced her curved lips with his fingertip, appearing fascinated by their shape and silky texture. "No. We are back to how you make me feel."

She wrapped her arms around him and wished she could hold him here with her forever. Wished that she could stop time. "That's better."

They stood that way, arms wrapped around each other, foreheads touching, for a long time. Finally, accepting the inevitable, Charity drew away, her eyes shimmering with tears. "I'm not going to say goodbye."

There was an ache in his throat so large Starbuck couldn't swallow. And there was an enormous gaping black hole where his heart used to be. "No. No goodbyes."

And then his mouth was on hers, covering and conquering and creating a deep, aching warmth. It was not a kiss meant to soothe or comfort. It was a kiss born of raw and turbulent emotions.

On a soft sob, her lips parted in irresistible and avid invitation. His mouth was fevered with desperation, his hands rough with urgency. Swearing, first in English, then switching to Sarnian, he plunged into the dark desperate kiss, boldly taking what he needed, heatedly giving what she needed in return.

And then, before he dragged her down to the floor, he released her.

Shaken, Charity stared up at him, wondering what kind of man possessed so much self-restraint he could put aside such fevered passion. Tense and wired and quivering like a plucked bowstring, she closed her eyes and struggled for control.

Then, she did the only thing possible. Biting her lip to keep from begging him to stay, she walked out of the lab. And out of Starbuck's life.

Dylan was waiting for her by the Jeep.

"You really love the guy, don't you, kiddo?" he asked, his dark blue eyes filled with sympathy.

"Of course I do." She took a deep breath and scrubbed impatiently at the tears streaming down her face with the back of her hands. "Enough to let him go."

"Does it help knowing that he loves you, too?"

She shook her head. "No. Oh, it probably will, one of these days," she decided reluctantly. "But right now, I don't think there's anything either you or Starbuck can say to make me feel better."

She lifted a hand to his cheek. "But, thank you, Dylan. You're a terrific brother."

Her decision made, and wanting to leave before she weakened and changed her mind, she climbed into the Jeep and drove back to her office.

SHE COULDN'T THINK. After arranging for the state police to come and take her prisoners, Charity put Andy in charge for the remainder of the day and went home.

Digging out her Grandmother Prescott's cookbook, Charity began to bake, hoping that the concentration such an endeavor demanded would keep her from thinking about Starbuck. From wondering if he made it safely back to Sarnia and hoping he'd remember her and what they'd shared, when he did.

Two hours later, the kitchen was filled with smoke, and all she had to show for her efforts were a stack of what looked like flat charcoal disks and a muffin tin of charred, heavy rocks.

Deciding that perhaps the birds might not be too choosy, she took the cookie sheets outside. That's when she saw him. Walking toward her in a strong, determined stride.

At first Charity couldn't believe it was really Starbuck. It was undoubtedly a hologram, like the ones he showed her he could create from his mind.

Dropping the cookie sheets into the snow, she ran toward him, hurling herself into his firm arms. This was no hologram, she realized, as he covered her face with kisses. The man she loved was wonderfully, gloriously real.

"I should say I'm sorry." Tears of happiness streamed down her uplifted face. "But I'm not."

He buried his lips in her fragrant hair. "Neither am I."

"What went wrong?"

"Nothing went wrong."

"But you wanted to go home, to prove your theory worked."

"It's enough for me to know that it works," Starbuck assured her. "As for going home, that's exactly what I've done."

He cupped her wet face in his hands. "All my life, I've struggled to be a proper Sarnian scientist. I've spent thirty years feeling like an outsider on my own planet, forced to suppress emotions that were inappropriate. But now, here, with you, for the first time in my life, I feel as if I'm exactly where I belong."

She traced the shape of his face. "For all time."

"For eternity," he agreed.

As they walked back toward the house, something occurred to her. "Poor Dylan must be devastated not to have had a chance to prove his theory."

"On the contrary. It went off like clockwork. In fact, your brother is undoubtedly having the time of his life."

"What?" Comprehension dawned. "Dylan's gone? To Sarnia?"

"There was only enough diamaziman for one," he reminded her.

The idea was almost too incredulous to take in. "Dylan on Sarnia. Two hundred years in the future." She shook her head. "You're right, he's probably in seventh heaven."

THE MOON HAD BEGUN to rise, casting a soft rosy glow over Sarnia. The inhabitants of the domed city were busy preparing for Truthfest, the annual observation of the arrival of the Ancient Ones. The two-week-long celebration was the one time in the year when even the most logical Sarnians, aided by vast amounts of Enos Dew, tended to loosen the reins on their emotions.

The commuters were already smiling in anticipation. Their thoughts focused on the upcoming days, they failed to notice the sparkling bits of matter reassembling themselves outside the quartzalite windows of their speeding air shuttles.

"It works!" Dylan stared around him in wonder. "Hot damn," he shouted, "it actually works!" He could feel the grin practically splitting his face in half.

A grin that faded when he realized that he was standing face-to-face with a pair of very large, very ugly men clad in black uniforms. They reminded him vaguely of Brian and Murph, although Vanessa's two henchmen had lacked the thick, leathery frontal ridge that ran along these men's foreheads. There was, however, the same primitive violence in their eyes.

"You're late," one of the men accused in a guttural language, which Starbuck's translator obligingly decoded.

Starbuck had assured Dylan that since English was
the chosen language of the terrans on Sarnia, he would
be able to make himself understood. "I got held up."

The men exchanged a look. "Truthfest is about to
begin. We get paid overtime for holidays."

"Well, I'm here now," Dylan pointed out.

With a shrug of his massive shoulders, the larger of
the two men punched a code into what resembled a solar pocket calculator. The door panel behind him slid
silently open. "Your prisoner awaits."

"Prisoner?"

Deciding that somehow he must have miscalculated
and landed somewhere other than Julianna Valderian's
home, Dylan entered the gleaming white building. The
door closed behind him, leaving him all alone in the
foyer.

He was not alone for long. Two more men, twins to
the pair outside the door, and dressed in identical uniforms and knee-high black boots, entered the room
with a rough, arrogant swagger. Between them was a
woman who could only be Julianna Valderian.

Starbuck had told Dylan that his sister was intelligent. And stubborn. As his appreciative gaze swept
over her, Dylan wondered why his friend had neglected
to mention her beauty.

Her hair was a gleaming silver, arranged in a braided
coronet atop her head. Her body was reed slender, but
from the way the silvery blue gown clung to her figure,
he could see that she had curves in all the right places.

Her eyes were a tawny topaz, revealing intelligence
and something else that strangely seemed to be disgust.

"So, you've finally arrived," she said. Her voice was
soft, but there was an edge to it Dylan didn't like.

"Everybody certainly seems concerned about punctuality around here," he complained. "And I think you've mistaken me for someone else."

"Oh, I know exactly who you are." Julianna held out her hands, revealing the steel bands that encircled her wrists. "You're the man who's come to escort me to my execution."

CHARITY AND STARBUCK were almost back at the house when something occurred to her. "I hate to ask this, but what if Dylan can't get back?" The thought was too horrendous to contemplate.

"He'll make it," Starbuck assured her with a cocky self-confidence that reminded her of her brother. "Julianna will help him. Besides, he's got a date back here in two weeks."

"What's happening in two weeks?"

"He's agreed to be best man at our wedding. We decided that would be sufficient time to notify your mother and bring her back from Tahiti for the ceremony."

"Did it occur to either of you two geniuses that no one thought to ask me if I wanted to get married?"

He stopped in his tracks, obviously surprised. "But you told me that you loved me."

"I do," she said quickly.

"And I love you." His brow was furrowed, a frustrated puzzlement darkened his eyes. "And we both agreed that we want to spend the rest of our lives together, so it was only logical to assume that you would want to get married."

The emotions were there, Charity knew. She could feel them, warm and deep and rich, flowing from his heart. But his Sarnian mind was still, and perhaps always would be, seeking logic, even in places there was none to be found.

After all, love, by its very nature, was illogical.

She did love him. All of him, his generous and caring heart, his body, even his sometimes frustrating, oftentimes intriguing mind.

"If you are worried about my ability to support you, you need not have any concern," Starbuck began, choosing his words carefully.

"What are you talking about?"

Obviously, Starbuck decided, eyeing her sudden scowl, that was not what had been keeping her from accepting his proposal.

"The man's duty is to provide for the family. That being the case, I want to assure you that I will be working with Dylan on future experiments. He tells me that the work will bring in enough grant money to enable me to care for a wife and children and I have no reason to doubt his accounting."

"Children?"

Starbuck never thought that Charity might not want to start a family. It only took him a fleeting second to decide that if all he were to have was her, it would be enough.

"I'm sorry. Am I taking too much for granted? About the children?"

"Not about the children," Charity assured him, moved by the honest regret she viewed in his eyes. "I've always wanted a family, Starbuck. And the idea of making babies with you is definitely appealing.

"But—" she crossed her arms "—I do not need a man to support me. I am perfectly capable of doing that by myself."

"You seem very self-sufficient," he agreed amiably.

"I am," she agreed with a brisk nod of her head. "And if I marry you, it will not be because I'm looking for a breadwinner. It will be because I love you."

"I understand." Starbuck was unreasonably concerned about the fact that she'd said *if* she married him. Not *when*.

"However," she continued, "I wouldn't mind at all if you wanted to take up the role of the bread *baker*."

He looked down at the charred crumbs scattered like chips of ebony over the white snow. The birds, chattering their disgust, pecked with obvious distaste at the results of two hours spent in a hot kitchen.

"I think," he decided, "that is the most logical idea you've come up with yet."

Charity laughed at that. She'd never been happier. Which was totally illogical, since her twin brother was currently hurtling through space, headed out of the galaxy.

Reminding herself that Dylan might be eccentric, but he wasn't crazy enough to attempt anything he wasn't truly positive would work, she decided to take Starbuck's word about her brother's safety.

Charity linked her arm through his. "Come on back to the house with me," she suggested. "We'll heat up some pizza in the microwave, and after dinner, you can spend the rest of the night convincing me of all the reasons I'm going to marry you."

"That scenario sounds most intriguing," Starbuck agreed. "Highly illogical, but definitely appealing."

"If you think that's illogical," Charity promised with a bold, sexy grin, "just wait until I introduce you to the wonders of bubble bath."

An erotic image shimmered between them. The sight of Charity clad in those frothy bubbles made his blood turn molten in his veins. "I think," Starbuck decided, "perhaps we should skip the pizza. To save more time for the bubble bath."

It made sense. After all, he tried telling himself, time management was a very logical science. Starbuck decided that anyone who would believe that his motive for foregoing dinner had anything to do with time management or logic would probably also be naive enough to buy swampland on the planet Floridiana.

"What a terrific idea." Charity's smile widened as she thanked the gods or fates or whatever destiny had brought this wonderful man all the way across space and time to her. "Who'd ever guess that logic could be so much fun?"

* * * * *

*Our intergalactic love story
continues next month in Temptation #436,*
MOONSTRUCK LOVERS.
*Dylan Prescott finds himself in
the adventure of a lifetime
when he helps Julianna Valderian flee
from the Sarnian forces
and discovers a woman worth fighting for.*

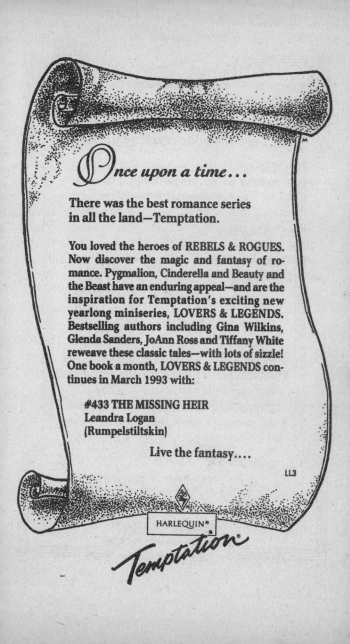

ᴼnce upon a time...

There was the best romance series
in all the land—Temptation.

You loved the heroes of REBELS & ROGUES.
Now discover the magic and fantasy of romance. Pygmalion, Cinderella and Beauty and
the Beast have an enduring appeal—and are the
inspiration for Temptation's exciting new
yearlong miniseries, LOVERS & LEGENDS.
Bestselling authors including Gina Wilkins,
Glenda Sanders, JoAnn Ross and Tiffany White
reweave these classic tales—with lots of sizzle!
One book a month, LOVERS & LEGENDS continues in March 1993 with:

#433 THE MISSING HEIR
Leandra Logan
(Rumpelstiltskin)

Live the fantasy....

LL3

HARLEQUIN®

Temptation

Harlequin is proud to present our best authors, their best books and the best for your reading pleasure!

Throughout 1993, Harlequin will bring you exciting books by some of the top names in contemporary romance!

In February, look for *Twist of Fate* by

Hannah Jessett had been content with her quiet life. Suddenly she was the center of a corporate battle with wealthy entrepreneur Gideon Cage. Now Hannah must choose between the fame and money an inheritance has brought or a love that may not be as it appears.

Don't miss TWIST OF FATE . . . wherever Harlequin books are sold.

Take 4 bestselling love stories FREE

Plus get a FREE surprise gift!

Special Limited-time Offer

Mail to Harlequin Reader Service®

3010 Walden Avenue
P.O. Box 1867
Buffalo, N.Y. 14269-1867

YES! Please send me 4 free Harlequin Temptation® novels and my free surprise gift. Then send me 4 brand-new novels every month, which I will receive before they appear in bookstores. Bill me at the low price of $2.44 each plus 25¢ delivery and applicable sales tax, if any.* I understand that accepting the books and gift places me under no obligation ever to buy any books. I can always return a shipment and cancel at any time. Even if I never buy another book from Harlequin, the 4 free books and the surprise gift are mine to keep forever.

142 BPA AJHR

Name	(PLEASE PRINT)	
Address	Apt. No.	
City	State	Zip

This offer is limited to one order per household and not valid to present Harlequin Temptation® subscribers.
*Terms and prices are subject to change without notice. Sales tax applicable in N.Y.

UTEMP-93

©1990 Harlequin Enterprises Limited